Comraich

Pauline K Murfin

Published by Pauline K Murfin

Pauline Murfin is a fifty nine year old mother, with three grown up sons. Married for thirty nine years to husband Graham, they live in a remote village in Northumberland.
Pauline and her husband Graham moved to a small village which is part of the Kielder Forest in the Northumberland National Park in 1999. Poor Health prevented Pauline from working, so she decided to study for a degree with The Open University. "To keep my brain ticking over", after completing her degree and gaining a Bachelor of Science she turns her hand to writing fiction. "Something I have always wanted to do" says Pauline.

Also by Pauline K Murfin

To Begin Again

This book is dedicated to my friends and family, without whose help, it could not have been written.

To my dear friend Elizabeth, thank you for spending many hours, correcting and proof reading, my atrocious spelling errors.

To Blanche for being totally supportive, in fact she is my own personal cheering section.

To Maxine my intrepid researcher in Manchester who is now a proud mum of a beautiful baby girl, Layla.

To Richard for his advice and technical knowledge on all things farm related.

To Graham without his technical ability my book would never get to print.

And Finally to Erik, who turns my raw manuscripts into the finished article, I am forever grateful.

Chapter 1

Kate was lying on a soft, fluffy, but very, very, cold bed – no, it can't be a bed, she thought, it's wet, what is it? Kate was struggling to pull her dulled senses into focus. Her mind was playing tricks on her. She could feel the warmth of something not unpleasant trickling slowly down her face, but her cheek felt as cold as ice. Kate tried to move to shake herself out of this dream which had now become uncomfortably real, too real, and she didn't like it.

Kate tried again to turn over and break the dream but a sharp pain made her shout out loud, or did she? Did any sound actually come out of Kate's mouth? She wasn't sure. She didn't really understand what was going on, and all she knew was that she needed to wake up. With a tremendous effort and all the will she could muster she let out a sound which started as a scream but came out more like a strangled moan, but she knew a sound had come out of her mouth because she felt her face lifted from the icy cold of the pillow. As her cheek left the ice cold surface, Kate suddenly realized she was not in bed and the pillow was not wet. It was snow and she was outdoors. With that realization she felt a tremendous pain in her head and somewhere in her chest, making her breath come in short, painful gasps. Kate could not take it in. Fear suddenly gripped her: where was she? What had happened? Had she had an accident? Oh god, she thought, the pain in her head making her almost unable to think, and really, she didn't want to think, she just wanted to go to sleep and hope it would all sort itself out in the morning.

Minutes later, when she opened her eyes again, even her eyes seemed not to want to open. Kate knew that this was not a dream and suddenly she was cold. She hadn't realized that she was shivering until her teeth banged together and woke her from her fitful slumber. Kate knew that this time she must try to stay awake and that it was not a dream ... but even as she thought about it she was slipping away into the dark abyss once more.

Kate stirred again and this time she was shivering in earnest, which was the only reason she had been able to pull herself from the deep slumber of contentment which was slowly sucking her under. She knew that she must attempt to move, stand up, do anything but lie there. She knew this, and yet it seemed the hardest thing in the world to hang on to those thoughts of urgency and actually do something about them.

Trying to move her limbs and find out what hurt and what didn't made Kate groan involuntarily, but she soon realized that her legs appeared to work, though the pain when she tried to make them work was excruciating. Trying to work out where the pain was coming from seemed too exhausting, and she had to stop and rest even from that simple effort. She became conscious of the fact that her chest hurt when she tried to breathe. She also realized that the warm feeling, which she had felt earlier, was blood – she tasted a smear from her fingers coming from somewhere on her head.

Her face seemed to be becoming tight – sort of lopsided, and she was having difficulty opening her left eye. Oh god, thought Kate, that's enough thinking for the moment, and she dropped her head back to the comfort of the cold, soft snow. That's when it dawned on Kate that there was something slowly coming down from the sky, which was silently, softly, and coolly landing on her face. When a flake of soft white snow landed on Kate's mouth and she tasted the wet coldness of it she knew she must make a tremendous effort or she would die out here on her own.

Kate gathered her strength and started to try to pull herself into a sitting position. The pain in her chest was so fierce she could not stand it and gasped in short bursts to fill her lungs, while not allowing the pain to grip her. With a strength she did not know she possessed she managed to get herself onto all fours, though quite what she was going to do from that position she didn't know. Regardless, it seemed like an achievement when she managed it. Now Kate's problem was how to get from that position into a standing one without having to breathe too deeply or move her head, which caused her to feel sick, sleepy, and dizzy, all at once.

She felt her way along the ground to see if she could actually feel a road, but everything was so deep in snow that Kate had no idea if she was on the pavement or the road. In fact, for all Kate knew, she could have been on a roundabout, she would have to think about that when her head was a little clearer.

The task at hand was to feel for something solid and grab hold of it, and that's exactly what she did. As luck would have it she found what she thought must be a road sign pole and she scrambled to sit up and lean against it. Once rested, her next task would be to stand up and read what it said. In the meantime, thought Kate, I will just rest for a minute.

In a deep fog somewhere in her dreams, Kate could hear a dog barking, barking and barking. Oh, she wished it would be quiet, it was making her head throb even more. But the barking became louder and louder until suddenly Kate was jolted into life with what felt like a hot, wet, soggy … yuck! What? Something was licking her face! With a sudden flash of consciousness Kate became aware that it was a dog: a real dog that was licking her face. A sudden flash of excitement went through Kate – where there was a dog there was usually a person. Oh god, she thought, I hope this is not a lamppost I'm leaning against and this dog is out for its nightly ablutions! That would be typical of my luck, thought Kate.

Kate tried to shout out for help but wasn't altogether sure how loud the words came out. She tried again: "HELP!" But it hurt her head and her face to shout and she was overcome with waves of sickness, and the sheer effort of calling was exhausting. She thought, I simply must close my eyes and lie still for a minute then I will shout again.

"Elsa, Elsa come here."

Kate thought she heard a distant voice calling, but not in an urgent way.

"Elsa!" more firmly this time, "come here – what are you doing you silly girl?"

Suddenly Kate could feel hot breath on her face, panting, licking, and a sort of rasping feel on her face. It was warm but sloppy. Kate was drifting in and out of consciousness when it suddenly came to her through a haze – she had not dreamt it, it was a dog! She wasn't afraid for some reason; she knew that the voice in the distance must be the owner of the hot breath and sloppy tongue.

She tried to shout but all that came out of her body was a pained groan.

"Elsa, what on earth are you doing?" said the disembodied voice, from what seemed a long way away. James was irritated by Elsa's lack of obedience, but at the same time he knew that Elsa would not disobey for no reason, so as he pulled on his wellington boots and coat to investigate whatever was so interesting that Elsa, a normally very well behaved German Shepherd, had found, and wouldn't leave until James also saw it.

James shined his powerful torch through the darkness and trudged through the soft, deep snow. He could hear Elsa making sounds of excitement – whatever it was she was really pleased with herself for finding it. As James got closer he thought he heard a moan. Kate in the meantime was trying to make herself heard, as she could hear the crunching of the snow as the person got closer. She knew this might be her only chance before the stranger went on his or her way. She moaned a sort of strangled shout and managed a sharp intake of breath, as the pain in her chest made her gasp. James heard the noise and went straight to where Elsa was sniffing.

"My God, Elsa! What the hell? You found a body!"

James knelt down to the prone figure and propped the torch close so he could take a look at what he had found and to see what injuries the woman had, as it was obvious that no one lay in the snow in the middle of nowhere unless they were injured: "Can you hear me," said James, firmly.

A moan confirmed that indeed the person had heard and was at least alive, though so much blood had seeped into a large pool on the pure white snow that he was almost afraid in case the body did not reply. The pool of blood appeared to be centered round the head area, and when trying to investigate closer, it became obvious that the body was that of a woman with long hair that was soaked in blood and wet snow, making it a sticky mass.

James tried to lift the woman into a sitting position and with that the woman let out a loud exhalation of breath. Realizing that she may have injuries which he could not see in the dark, or until he could get her into the farm and assess the damage, James lay her down again.

"Guard," he instructed Elsa.

Elsa was like a typical mother watching over her puppy: no way would she leave her find. James said to the semi-conscious woman, "Don't worry, I won't be long. Elsa will stay with you."

As he made to stand up, a weak hand came out and attempted to hang on to his sleeve.

"I'm just going to get the jeep, don't worry I will come back," and with that he hurried off back towards the barn. James decided on the quad, which already had the flatbed trailer attached, as he had just got back from dropping hay to the cows in a field nearby. The flatbed would probably be easier to lay the woman on, especially if she were in great pain, he couldn't, very well, haul her into the land rover. He drove carefully but quickly over the deep snow, and was soon back to the gate, which Kate had been leaning against, which she had believed to be some sort of road sign. If she only but knew that she must have found the only solid post in fifty miles as she was nowhere near a main road.

James opened the gate and went to lift the woman from where she was leaning. Elsa was lying against her as if to keep her warm.

"Good girl Elsa, now let me in," he said as he knelt down to the prone figure, speaking in a very firm and confident voice.

"I'm going to lift you up," he warned, "it may hurt a little, but you will have to try to grit your teeth, because I have to get you on to the trailer. Do you hear me?"

The girl moaned, so James lifted her up. With his considerable strength it was not hard, the hard part was trying not to hurt her, as he did not yet know what was wrong; however, his instincts told him that something was terribly wrong.

James had thrown an old horse blanket hastily on the trailer and he lay Kate down and covered her with the blanket, directing, "Elsa up," to the anxious dog, and Elsa immediately jumped up and took her place next to Kate. Somehow Kate felt the warmth of the dog's body and took comfort in it. Kate seemed to gasp over every bump in the ground, even though the snow had made the ground fairly even. It was so deep she still bounced up and down on the flat surface of the trailer.

James soon arrived at the door of the farm house, and he told the woman to get ready, as he was about to lift her into the house. He assured her that this would be the last move and she would be all right after that, which is the kind of thing you say to reassure people, whether it's true or not.

It was tricky getting down from the trailer and then lifting Kate to the edge without hurting her too much but in the end he had to harden his heart, as he did when looking after a sick animal, and just go for it. He took firm hold of Kate and closed his ears to her cries of pain.

Kicking the heavy door open a pool of light spilled out and he got his first glimpse of the figure he carried. It was definitely a woman, but he had already guessed as much by the mass of long hair. Her face was so covered in blood and bruised he could not at first be sure. James went straight to the large leather sofa in front of the log burning stove and lay Kate down, shouting at the same time, "Izzy, Izzy, come here …"

Footsteps came running down the wooden stairs and a young girl appeared.

Chapter 2

The girl was about seven or eight with olive coloured skin, huge, dark eyes and shiny, black hair. She was not unlike the cherubs often depicted by old masters, with the fattest curls which frame their chubby faces. She stopped halfway down the stairs and looked through the banister to see her father leaning over something lying on the sofa. It was not unusual for her dad to bring an injured animal into the house, and it wouldn't be the first time he had brought a young calf that was ill or new born lambs to warm them. However, as Izzy moved closer, she could see this was not a calf or a lamb, it was a woman! She hurried to the sofa as James was pushing a cushion under Kate's head.

"Get me a bowl with some warm water, a facecloth, and a towel. Then can you help me get her boots off? Oh and can you fetch me a blanket and pillow from the bedroom?" said James. "Good girl, as quick as you can."

Izzy brought the blanket and pillow first, then the bowl of warm water and the towel while her father was busy trying to see where the blood was coming from. It was obvious that the bruising on the woman's face was coming from her right eye, which was rapidly closing from an obviously tremendous blow of some sort. That was not, however, where the blood was coming from. He carefully examined her head with his probing fingers until she suddenly gasped in pain, and James knew he had found the source of the blood.

Upon closer inspection she had a massive swelling on the left side of her head and a gash which was causing the heavy bleeding. The wound was quite deep and at least three inches in length, but James felt slightly happier once he could see where all the blood was coming from – at least he could see it and would be able to treat it, and had it been internal that would have been a different story.

"Izzy, we've got to get her coat and boots off to make her more comfortable. Can you hold this cloth firmly against her head to stem the flow of blood? I'll try to get her jacket off."

Izzy took hold of the towel and pressed it firmly against the woman's head while James struggled with the woman's jacket. Kate gasped in pain as James started to remove her coat, and it became obvious that there was another injury in that area. Being as gentle as he could, James managed to get her coat off, but he couldn't see anything visible. As he gently probed down Kate's ribs there was a sudden sharp gasp of pain, and it became clear to James that it was a rib and hopefully it was only the one. He needed to find out if she had any other injuries, so he continued his examination, as he gently went down her legs he was almost certain that it was only her rib cage that hurt, along with the gash on her head, not to mention the black eye which by now was closed and very colourful.

James took a deep breath and looked at Izzy who, although doing exactly what she had been instructed too, was naturally wondering where on earth her father had found this woman: they lived twenty miles away from the nearest village, never mind town.

"Well, Izzy, I don't know where she came from," said James absently, "but she's hurt and needs help." He looked at his watch.

"Eight thirty. There's no way any doctors surgery would be open now, and the snow is really coming down," said James.

It had snowed for days and it was at least a foot deep on the main road, but there were drifts of up to four feet in certain places, as their farm was very high up. James took a deep breath and said to Izzy, "Well, Izzy, my dear girl, you and me are going to have to play doctor and nurse, okay?"

"Of course," Izzy said gravely to her dad. Izzy thought of her dad as kind of brilliant at times like this. She actually thought he was rather a dish compared to other girl's dads, but in a crisis he was a 'super-hero'.

"Right, Izzy, we need to get her clothes off the best we can so I can at least strap her ribs. We have some strapping left that we got for Merlin's foal in the barn; can you get that while I get the first-aid box?"

Once they had everything they needed, James got Kate's heavy snow boots off and loosened her trousers and tried to lift Kate's weight off the material while Izzy pulled them off. Kate moaned, wishing whoever it was would stop jiggling her about and leave her alone. She was warm and cozy now and just wanted to sleep and sleep. Much to her relief, she could soon feel a lovely warm blanket being tucked around her and a soft voice saying to her from a distance that she was going to be all right now, but that something was going to hurt a bit. Then she was being lifted into a sitting position and she screamed with the sharp pain in her rib cage.

James told Izzy to put her weight behind Kate and keep her in an upright position while he strapped around her ribs with the broad strapping he had got for the foals young legs when they were too weak to hold her up. He tied as tight as he dared without cutting off her air supply, then they gently let her lie back down and covered her up.

Taking a good look at the gash on the top of her head, James decided that if it was a horse he would clean the cut then suture it, so that's exactly what he would do. Izzy cut the strips of elastoplast tape and he cleaned the wound. God, it was deep, thought James. It really needed stitching properly, but he could only do his best and see what the weather was like in the morning and hopefully attempt to take her to a hospital.

In the meantime James tried to close the gash with his finger while Izzy placed the strips over it, which was difficult as the area was sticky and her hair was thick.

Izzy tutted and said, "Dad, I hate to cut her hair, but I can't stick the strips unless I cut some of it away…"

So with the little scissors from the box, Izzy carefully cut away a little area for the strips of tape to stick to. After placing the single strips across the deep cut, they put a large plaster over the top to keep it all in place and gently lay Kate's head back on the pillow.

Izzy gently washed Kate's face with the warm water taking care not to put any pressure anywhere near her swollen eye, but also needing to see if there were any other injuries that they had not seen through the sticky blood which was rapidly drying all over Kate's face. Izzy said she didn't think there were any cuts and that it was just the blood from her head.

Izzy added, "Doesn't she look as though she would be quite pretty if she hadn't got such a massive swelling round her eye?"

Izzy said this to her father who was standing up now looking very pensively at the prone figure of the woman he had just found in the middle of a snow storm, miles from anywhere, and with injuries which were suited to a bar room brawl, never mind any car accident that he had come across. He could see that she was slim and probably about five foot five or so, with long black curly hair. But it was difficult to imagine her face, as it was streaked with blood, and as Izzy said, she was going to have a heck of a shiner for a while.

"Who is she dad, where did you find her?"

"Ask Elsa," he answered, "she found her lying against the gate post in the snow. The question now is what the heck do we do with her? I didn't really see if she had anything with her to say who she is. I will have to look in the morning, when it's light. My immediate concern is, do we let her sleep or not? In a case of concussion, which I'm sure she's got, to say the least, I think you are supposed to keep the person awake. But I'm only guessing, I don't really know. It would seem cruel when she is so obviously in need of rest."

James mused, pulling a face at Izzy, "It's amazing what your dog will bring home with her, Izzy, she couldn't just bring a rabbit home like other dogs…"

And they both laughed which released some of the tension they had both felt for the last half an hour. James put more logs on the stove and said, "If you sit with her for a little while, I will go and check the stock, settle Tip down, and lock up, then I will decide what to do about sleeping beauty here, okay?"

Tip was their working border collie who slept in the barn and more or less guarded the outside animals just as Elsa, Izzy's German shepherd, watched the inside brood, Izzy and James. When James came back, via the boot room, shaking off the snow and kicking off his boots, he shouted to Izzy, "Well, there is nobody coming or going outside tonight, the snow is really coming down now. There is nothing for it but to let her sleep and we will see what the morning brings."

"She seems to have skiing clothes on Dad – you know, the jacket and her boots are for skiing. But how on earth did she get to our farm, it's nowhere near the ski slope?"

"I think you're right Izzy, it does look like skiing gear. But again, how on earth did she get here, and what's happened to her? The more I look, the less I think she has been in an accident. It's much more likely she has been punched, with her eye the way it is, and she's fallen and cracked her head and ribs. Anyway, I think you should go off to bed and I will just make sure she is comfortable. I'll leave Elsa with her and Elsa can come to me if she stirs in the night."

"Okay, night Dad," Izzy stopped and said through the wooden banister. "Who would have thought it, Dad, Santa has sent you a woman for Christmas!" And with that Izzy went upstairs, laughing at her own joke and thinking how nice it was to have another person in the house, even though she loved the life her and her father had together. She had to admit that this was exciting.

It was almost as exciting as Christmas, which was only three days away.

James stood watching the mysterious woman before deciding that he would not go upstairs to bed, but just doze in the armchair in case she woke up and was scared of Elsa, although it was quite obvious that Elsa was totally smitten with her role as foster mother.

After turning out the lamps James eventually went into an exhausted doze. The only light was that of the flames from the log burner flickering on the ceiling and the twinkling of the tree lights on the huge fresh Christmas tree in the corner.

Chapter 3

The night went over without incident except for Kate's call of nature; it's amazing how the body knows what to do even when practically unconscious. Once James had brought her back from the downstairs shower room and toilet, normally only used by himself after working on the farm all day, he settled her back down on the sofa then asked her quietly and gently, "What is your name?"

"Kate," came back the sleepy reply.

"Where are you from?"

"Manchester."

"Manchester?" asked James in a louder, more astonished voice.

It was becoming obvious that Káte, the mysterious woman who now had a name, was probably here on a skiing holiday and somehow ended up lost. James sat thinking about this for awhile then must have dozed fitfully before waking up stiff and tired from sleeping in the chair, realizing it was time to go out on the farm and start feeding the animals. A quick look out of the boot room window told him that a lot more snow had fallen during the night and no one would be going anywhere today. Putting on his waterproof coat and wellington boots he went off to start the round of feeds. James loved this work and had never regretted giving up his job as a journalist in favour of taking over the farm from his parents; however, on mornings like this, when it was still pitch dark and it was cold and wet, he would normally feel the pull of his warm bed. Today, however, was different on so many levels: he was in a hurry to get through his work, so that he could get back to Kate and to see how she was this morning. He could hardly wait to find out a little more about where and how she come to be sitting against his front gate in the middle of a snow storm. Like Izzy, he thought it was nice to have another person in the house, especially a woman, even though she was shrouded in mystery.

As soon as James entered the big barn, where the rows of cows and calves were noisily waiting to be fed, Tip was instantly at his side. James thought, farming is farming and I love it, whatever the weather. It took him a couple of hours to shovel out the shed floors and put feed in the troughs for those cows which he had brought over in October and had now calved. In the next barn he had fifty Kylies which had also calved in October. People think of these cows by the long horns making them look like something off the American cattle ranch; Kylies and Galloways are very well suited to the Scottish weather which often goes to minus nineteen in the hardest part of winter. All the cows in the barns had recently calved but would normally stay out no matter what the weather.

James went out in the pickup to check on his sheep and dump silage in the troughs and make sure the water trough wasn't frozen. Many of the ewes were in lamb and James would bring them in around January to make sure they were well fed and at their best for delivering lambs in the spring. When James was out, he drove toward the farm gate and jumped out of the truck, with Tip not far behind, and he started to search around to see if he could find any signs of how Kate had arrived. Obviously tyre tracks were out of the question, because of the amount of snow that had fallen overnight, but he may find something else – some other clue.

It was Tip, actually, who started to dig in the snow, and James knew that something must be there, as collies could smell anything that shouldn't be there from a mile away. When James went over Tip had already uncovered what looked to be a suitcase.

Tip and James looked around the same area and he then came across a woman's handbag. This was becoming more and more intriguing. A quick search in the heavy snow led James to think he had probably got the most important things, so he headed back to the farm.

***

Kicking off his wellington boots and wet coat in the boot room, which was lovely and warm as it had a large Aga stove which fed the central heating system and kept everything warm as toast, James was more than ready for his morning coffee, as was his normal routine; however, this morning he crept into the living room to see how his patient was.

She appeared to be still asleep, but as he opened the heavy curtains, and tried to rake the ashes out of the log burner without giving her a fright, Kate's eyes suddenly flew open – well, one of them did, and the one that was swollen was the most beautiful shade of blue and purple would definitely remain closed for the day. The open eye just looked startled,

"Morning," said James, concernedly.

"Erm, morning. Erm … I'm sorry, I don't really…" and as Kate tried to sit up and speak, at the same time, her breath was caught in a sharp pain.

"Don't try to do anything," said James. "I don't know how much you remember but I found you outside in the snow, and I think you have a cracked or broken rib. You also have a really nasty cut on your head."

Kate immediately tried to feel the cut with her probing fingers and made herself wince and cry out, gasping for breath at the same time. As she tried to rub the sleep out of her eyes, she suddenly winced again, and James said, "Oh, and you have the most corking black and blue eye. Do you remember how you got to this farm? Did you have a car crash? Was there more than one of you?"

"Farm…" said Kate. "I'm on a farm?"

"Yes, did you not know that?"

"No. To be honest, I'm not sure what I know. I can't think."

Kate tried to look up from her prone position to see who it was she was talking to, but even that action hurt her head. The man was obviously very tall, because his jean clad legs seemed to go on forever. He was slim, because she could see his fancy belt buckle, as the cowboys wear, and he didn't have any excess stomach bulging over it. But other than that it was just a voice, a rather nice voice though she thought.

"Look," James said, "I'm going to make coffee and breakfast, could you eat anything?" James looked enquiringly at Kate, who had started to look at her body and where she was, on the sofa, wrapped in a blanket. She knew she had a jumper on and underclothes, but knew instinctively that she had no trousers on.

"Where are my trousers? And who…"

"Oh, don't worry, your trousers are here. And I wasn't alone – my daughter and I took your trousers and boots off. You were quite safe. You're in luck – we found what I presume to be your suitcase and handbag. They were buried in the snow near where I found you. Would you like me to take them to the shower room, and you could have a shower and change your clothes, if you think you can manage."

Kate attempted to nod and instantly regretted it. "Yes," she murmured instead, "I'll manage."

She made to stand up and wrap the blanket around her and gave a sharp gasp of pain as her ribs protested at the sudden movement. Trying to hold her head up and the blanket around her and not move her body around the chest area was proving to be very tricky, but she would do it even if it killed her. She needed to be in a room on her own so she could try to make sense of this whole situation.

James led the way and pointed to the downstairs bathroom, which he only he used after working on the farm. However, it was fairly clean and tidy, and very, very warm. James had already carried Kate's suitcase in and put it on top of the old wooden dresser in the bathroom, where they kept the fresh towels and toiletries. Kate thanked him and shut the door behind him after a quick instruction on how the shower worked. Kate slumped down on the side of the bath, rather heavily, and tried to take a deep breath in order to gather her thoughts. She winced in pain, mentally reminding herself that she must remember not to make any sudden movements again.

All right, she thought, it's obvious I've had some sort of accident and all I have to figure out now is how I got to this 'farm' and where the car is. Kate was aware of a nagging cramp in her stomach, which had made her feel even more uncomfortable at night, when she had tried her best to get comfortable on the sofa, where she was essentially warm and cozy.

Deciding instead on a hot bath, Kate turned the water on in the large bath and started to undress. While the bath was filling she opened her suitcase, and in among her clothes, which appeared to have been hastily thrown into it, she spotted a large box of tampons. As she stared at the box, slowly and through a haze of recollection, it began to come to her that she had thought she wouldn't need them but she would pack them anyway. Kate began to climb into the big, deep, old-fashioned, claw-footed bath. She moved very gingerly, as every part of her body hurt.

Her escalating pain was why she had decided on a bath instead of a shower, and thought maybe after the bath she would feel better and more able to understand what had happened to her. As she lay down in the warm bath water, her eyes closed, and she began to relax a little. If she hadn't had a terrible cramp in her stomach it would certainly have helped.

When Kate opened her eyes, with total horror, she saw the bath water turning blood red. As she stared at the water it came to her in a blinding flash: she wouldn't have needed the tampons because she was pregnant...

***

She remembered doing a test the day before she was due to go on her romantic, week long, skiing holiday with Dominic. She had placed the clear blue stick tester into the box of tampons and she would show Dominic when they were settled. She had been so excited, bursting to tell him, but she had kept her secret bottled up, she intended to wait until they were inside the ski lodge, in front of a roaring fire, with a glass of wine, and then tell him the wonderful news.

As Kate looked down into her bath to see the new life, which would have been no bigger than a fifty pence piece, ebb away, it all became clear. The whole awful scene began to play back like a video playing in her mind.

Chapter 4

From somewhere deep within her Kate made a sound which could only be described as primeval. As the sound began to erupt to her upper body, Kate grabbed a towel, which was the first thing that came to hand, and pushed it into her face to try to smother the sound which she knew was about to come out of her mouth. With the heart rending sob and gasp for breath, there was a tumult of feelings, of not only pain from her injuries, but the realization of what had happened. At this moment she could not put all the pieces together, but she was now fully aware that she had lost her baby. Her precious gift of life which she had hoped would cement her love for Dominic and his love for her.

Kate sobbed into the towel until she thought pain could not get any worse than this. She wasn't sure how long she sat there, sobs wracking her body, until eventually she felt numb from head to toe. Then something stirred inside her and she knew that she could not sit in the, now cooling, bath water. She must try to gather her thoughts. A knock on the door, asking tentatively if she was all right, pulled her tortured thoughts back to the present, and she rallied her voice enough to reply: "Yes, I'm fine, just trying to get my clothes on, I won't be long."

"Oh don't hurry, take all the time you need. I just wondered if you needed any help... Oh, I mean, not from me... I could get Izzy, my daughter, she would help you," James said a halting voice sounding a little unsure and slightly embarrassed.

"No, no, I will be ok," said Kate, trying to sound brave, but by now beset by feelings of the worst kind of desolation. She tried to stop the sobs, which were even now, as she was attempting to get dressed, still desperate to burst out of her, until she could have screamed with the need to just let the dam burst, and cry and cry until she was empty.

The practicalities of her situation helped her concentrate for a moment on the simple things like bending down to put on her panties: the pain in her chest seemed to explode every time she tried to lean over from the waist. That done eventually, it was obvious she would not be able to put the strapping back on, which James had put on to hold her together, more or less, and give her ribs some support.

She attended to her bra, gasping with the sheer effort of simply putting on underclothes; Kate slumped on to the side of the bath until she was able to carry on. She set about pulling on the first thing that came to hand out of the suitcase, which was a thick, warm, natural colour, polo neck sweater, and then a pair of jeans. The jumper was not so difficult once she pulled it over the first hurdle of the gash on her head, which caused her to cry out; then over her face, which she was until then unaware, had a massive swelling on her eye, and again winced loudly. She continued the struggle to pull it on her body, but the jeans were going to be a whole new ball game, she thought, with as deep a sigh as she could manage. At that moment another knock came tentatively on the door and James said again, "I'm sorry to pester you, but can you manage? Izzy is here and would really like to help you. I won't come in at all; she will come in on her own."

Kate decided that there was no point in being brave when all it would take was for someone to help her get her jeans on and some warm socks.

"Thank you," Kate shouted through the closed door. "You're very kind. And yes, I could do with some help."

As she hadn't locked the door, thankfully she did not have to move, and she could gather her strength. The door opened slowly and somewhere in her confused thoughts she seemed to recognize the beautiful cherubic face that peered around the door with her warm dark eyes and tentative smile, making Kate once again want to cry for no apparent reason. Kate's eyes were swimming with tears and at that moment the little girl put her hand on Kate's arm and said, "Don't worry, I won't hurt you," and Kate gave a sort of stifled laugh and a watery smile.

Kate knew instantly that she was going to like this little girl and the same thought had entered Izzy's mind as she started to help the pretty lady with the big black eye with her jeans and socks. Izzy said, in a very conspiratorial way, not to worry about the tidying up, and Kate just loved her for her thoughtfulness. When they had completed Kate's jeans and socks, Izzy, in a very grown up way, took Kate's arm and led her through to the large kitchen table where her father had laid a place for Kate to attempt to eat and drink something.

"Hi, I'm James," said the very tall figure with the nice voice, which Kate had heard earlier and now could actually put a face to. Her first thought was that he looked like a cowboy: long, lean, but certainly not mean. He had a weather tanned face which made his blue eyes glow and his teeth white as he smiled at her.

"You won't remember me, and this is Izzy, short for Isabella, my daughter." Izzy smiled at Kate then left to tidy the bathroom for her as she had promised.

James held out his hand for Kate to shake and she started to say, "Hello, I'm…"

"Kate," said James, "I established that much. And you are from Manchester?"

Kate half laughed, and said yes, with a questioning look.

"Before any explanations, can I just point out that the strapping you had bound around you was the best I could do to hold what I think may be a cracked, bruised, or even broken, rib in place, so my advice to you is that you allow me to put it back on for a day or two until we can get you somewhere for an x-ray. I don't think we will be able to get you an x-ray until after Christmas. Tomorrow is Christmas Eve, and in case you haven't remembered, there is an awful lot of snow out there, too much even for my truck to get you to somewhere like Aberdeen or Edinburgh."

"Oh no! You mean I'm stuck here until after Christmas?! Oh, I'm sorry. I didn't mean that the way it sounded, only, I need … I need…" and then with a sob she hadn't realized she still had in her, she said, "Oh, I don't know what I need! Everything hurts, and…"

Kate's voice trailed away. She wasn't sure what to say – she didn't know this person from Adam and she felt as though she were about to spill her whole sad story to him.

The truth was she didn't really know the whole story; she hadn't worked it out yet. She remembered the argument with Dominic, and the fact that he had become more and more furious until he began pushing her; she remembered his exact words after she told him how wonderful it was going to be with the baby and everything: he had stared her straight in the face and shouted with unmistakable venom: "I don't own the bloody office, I just work there!" Then as he turned he said over his shoulder, "That is, if I still have a job..." which seemed to make his temper erupt again and turn toward Kate and begin pushing her with every point he made: "How could we afford a baby? How could you be so stupid? Who said I wanted a baby?"

And then Kate tried to calm him down, saying all the things that one does in a situation that needed calming.

"Don't worry, I will be working. I'll just take maternity leave then go back to work," though Kate had always wanted to be a full time mum, if ever the time came, but needs come first when the situation warrants it.

"It won't cost that much, and you will love it, once it comes... I know it's probably earlier than we would have liked, but..."

Dominic's face went ominously white and he grabbed hold of Kate's face and spat the words out so close she could feel his breath, hot and wet.

"What don't you understand? I do not want you, or your baby. I do not want to see you again, and I want you out of my life, do you understand?"

As Dominic started to release Kate's chin she said,
"Dominic, you don't mean that, you are just shocked." The words had hardly left her mouth when Dominic lifted the back of his hand and lashed out at her face with a blow that was so powerful it lifted her off her feet. She went down with her head landing against the hearth, cracking her head open and rendering her unconscious. Kate had no further recollection of what happened next.

Kate realized that she had been sat at the table and James was obviously waiting for some sort of response from her, but she had no idea what.

"I'm sorry, what did you ask me? I'm not really with it."

"No you're not. And you should not be sitting here at the table; come on, let's get you back on the sofa, and I will bring you something to eat and drink. But first I'll get the strapping for your ribs. Do you want Izzy to be here while I do it? I can assure you I am totally honorable and I don't usually have to resort to rendering a woman incapable before making my move," said James with a wry smile.

Kate tried a smile and said, "Just do your worst, and I'm sorry if I seem like a wimp, I will try not to cry."

"Izzy, your daughter, she is gorgeous, what a face! She will break some boys' hearts; does she take after her mother?" Kate, though telling the truth, was trying to keep herself distracted from the fact that a man she didn't know was as close as a man could get without it being sexual.

"Oh, thank you, is that a way of saying that I am obviously not the source of her good looks?" laughed James, who was also trying to keep up the banter, while strapping something other than a calf or a foal.

"Oh, sorry, I didn't mean that, I just thought…"

"Yes, I know. Actually she is very much like her mother was."

"Oh, I'm terribly sorry, I shouldn't have pried. I didn't mean to…"

"No, no, she isn't dead. We are divorced. And it was a long, long time ago, when Izzy was a toddler. Ok, finished. It's not perfect, but I think it will support your rib until we can get you to an x-ray, however, I don't honestly know when that will be. The weather is the worst I have ever seen at this time of the year and shows no signs of letting up. Tomorrow is Christmas Eve and I would imagine it will be a skeleton staff over Christmas. I rang the NHS direct help line last night and described your symptoms, and without seeing you they could not be sure, but they think it could be a badly bruised rib or even a crack. Would you believe they apparently don't do much other than strap you nowadays? So, if we're lucky, the strapping will be enough. They said to take pain killers every four hours. The best I have is Paracetamol, which they said would be fine, so you could take two now, which should ease the pain a little."

"Honestly, I don't think there is any need for hospital treatment, I'm sure I'm just bruised," said Kate, not really wanting to answer any awkward questions thrown at her by the hospital staff. "I am just so grateful that I managed to find my way here," and her voice tailed off as she lowered her eye contact with James. She didn't know why, but for some reason, she wasn't ready to tell him the truth. Or maybe she simply wasn't ready to actually believe the truth: that, somehow, she had been dumped outside this farm. Otherwise what would explain the fact that her baggage was with her? If you have a car crash, your luggage doesn't fall out of the boot before the car disappears.

James let it rest, as he could see she was uncomfortable when it came to the details of her appearing at his farm gate. He was sure that the story would unfold in time. He helped Kate through to the living room and she lay back down on the sofa. With the curtains now open to the large picture window, it was the first time that she had seen exactly how much snow had fallen.

"Oh my god, look at the snow! Where did all that come from?"

The view out of the window showed a complete white out, except what she supposed were the fence posts, strung from either side of the gate in the distance, which you could only see the tops of. She could see, to the side of the farm house, three large barns, and the snow was piled high, making them look like giant loaves of bread. Only one set of tracks showed in the deep snow, and that she supposed, were James' tracks, where he had been out to feed his cattle.

At that moment a sudden loud noise made her jump. Kate jerked round, heart thumping, and gave a sharp intake of breath. It was only James raking the stove out and putting more logs on the fire. Kate had never been a nervous person, but for some reason she seemed to be a bundle of nerves. She knew that she was out of her depth, lost, frightened, and at a total loss as to what to tell this kind man and his daughter. They had come to her rescue, and to all intent and purpose, saved her life. This was undeniable, even accepting only the simple fact that, had she lain out there in the snow all night, by morning, she would have been dead.

James came to her rescue in the midst of these desolate thoughts, once again."

"Right, I know you probably don't feel like it, but I'm going to make you some breakfast and coffee. I'm sure you must be starving by now. I sure as hell am. What can I get you? Bacon? Eggs? Scrambled eggs?"

Just at that moment Izzy came into the room, and James said to his daughter, "I do a mean breakfast, don't I, Izzy?"

"He makes a lucious breakfast, Kate. Do you mind me calling you Kate?" asked Izzy, inquiringly, just as though she were talking to a friend of her own age.

Kate answered, "Only, if I can call you Izzy."

"Oh! Everyone calls me Izzy. And, if I were you, I would have the scrambled eggs, the eggs are fresh from my own chickens," she said with great pride.

"You have your own chickens? Aren't you lucky! I've always wanted to keep chickens, but there is no way I could keep them, in the city…"

"My chickens are… well, I have two types of chickens: I specialize in Scots Grey miniatures and Scots Dumpy miniatures."

This was said with absolute seriousness, and as Kate lifted her eyes to meet James' eyes, his look confirmed his daughter's statement, and with a certain amount of pride he said, "Izzy has won prizes for her hens, haven't you, Izzy?"

"Yes, both Henry and Henrietta have had firsts in the agricultural show in Tillykerrie, and Willaby and Willamina got a very creditable second last year, and they are only one year old, so I have great hopes for them this year!"

This all said with such seriousness and with no false pride it could only be taken one way: that Izzy was indeed very proud of her own achievements, and James was equally proud of his daughter.

"Then how can I refuse? It's eggs for me, thank you very much…" Kate said, trying to join in James' and Izzy's attempt to cheer this very unhappy lady up. Izzy showed her eggs to Kate before James started to scramble them, and Kate was actually amazed.

"They're cream! How lovely, how unusual! Are they always that colour?"

"Oh yes," said Izzy, in a very knowledgeable way, making it clear that hens were definitely Izzy's thing, and not just something she did as a chore on the farm.

James gave Kate two painkillers and a coffee and left, saying he would be back with breakfast in two shakes, and leaving Kate snuggled up on the sofa with the blanket wrapped around her and the heat from the roaring log fire warming her cheeks. As Kate looked out of the window, seeing the constant blowing of the snow, which was almost horizontal and showed no signs of ever letting up, it became clear that she would have to come to terms with the fact that she would not be getting any answers to her nightmare for quite a while yet. It also became clear that she would have to spend this time trying to heal this unbearable feeling of rawness inside of her, not to mention her physical state of disrepair, she thought wryly.

A bruised or cracked rib, a massive gash in her head, which made touching her head painful – never mind washing or combing her hair – and a black eye that had shocked her, making her step back rapidly from the mirror as she caught sight of it in the bathroom. All this would be answered in the fullness of time, she told herself silently. And whatever had happened to Dominic to make him turn into…

"Here we go, eggs a la Izzy," said James, as he came in carrying a tray with Kate's breakfast on, closely followed by Izzy. James put the tray on Kate's knees and Izzy came round him to put a tiny little Christmas tree on the tray, which had been made from a little branch of their tree with a little piece of tinsel draped over it and put into an egg cup.

"And a merry Christmas," said Izzy, her voice full of excitement. It had occurred to Izzy that this woman was not going anywhere in this weather, so not only was Christmas only a day away, but her father and she were not going to be alone this year after all. James' parents always came for Christmas ever since Jennifer had left, his mother claiming a child needed a woman at

Christmas. But this year James' father, or Grandpa Andy, as Izzy called him, had been really doing poorly. He had a real bout of flue, which had turned to a chest infection, and for the first time in his life he was bed bound, which he did not take kindly to. Grandma Ailsa was fussing over him like a mother hen, he had told Izzy when she spoke to him on the phone: "Like your Henrietta!" and they had both laughed, imagining Grandma as Henrietta.

Kate was overwhelmed by the kindness of this wonderful man and his beautiful little girl, how lucky she had been to be found by them.

Chapter 5

Kate felt comfortably stuffed with the wonderful tasting breakfast and suitably numbed by the pain killers and without realizing it she had dozed off again. When she awoke, something told her it was late afternoon as the light was fading. She could see that it must have snowed most of the day, but as it became darker Kate could see the snow begin to glisten, which meant the temperature had plummeted and it was now freezing.

She got out from under her blanket and decided she must make a supreme effort to be normal in some way. She folded the blanket and went to switch on the table lamps in the room. She presumed that James must be out working in that freezing weather, so she thought she would put some logs on the fire so that it looked inviting for him coming in. It took her a while to figure out how the doors opened on the log burner, and she then knelt down, which was easier than trying to bend; bending over was strange, it was as though she had a plaster cast on and could not move.

After putting some logs on the fire and putting the lamps on, it suddenly seemed darker outside, so she drew the curtains. She found her way through to the kitchen, which she had been in briefly this morning, and where she found the source of a wonderful smell, which had been filling the air since she woke.

She went on a little tour to see the lay of the land, so to speak. It was a strange feeling not knowing where you are on the outside, never mind inside. She found the bathroom, which (bless her heart) Izzy had tidied for her, and put Kate's scattered clothes in a neat pile on top of her suit case. The bathroom was at the end of the boot room, which was exactly what the name implied: where all the outdoor clothing and the dog's bed were kept, which reminded her she had not seen the massive dog that seemed to have been her constant companion, and by all accounts, was responsible for saving her life.

Just then the back door burst open with loud voices and feet being kicked against the step to remove excess snow. Exaggerated shivers could be heard as James, Izzy, and Elsa came bursting in out of the cold night. Elsa came straight over to where Kate was leaning against the table and snuffled Kate with her long nose, wagging her tail excitedly.

"Elsa, Elsa," James said hurriedly, in case Kate was afraid of the over-sized mutt.

"Please, don't worry, I am not afraid. I owe my life to this huge bundle of fur, and anyone can see she is not in the least dangerous."

"Ha!" said James loudly. "If she didn't know you and like you, and you were standing here in her kitchen, by now you would be on the floor and she would be sitting on you until I called her off. But she has decided that you are her responsibility, and you have no idea how hard it has been keeping her out of the house while you had some rest."

"Hi," said Izzy. "Are you feeling any better? I popped in before I did the chickens, but you were fast asleep."

"I feel much better, thank you Izzy. I feel embarrassed. I had that lovely breakfast, then I must have dozed off. I feel such a lazy person when both you and your dad are out working in this weather."

At this point, James said that what she needed was rest, and that the best thing for healing was sleep. After depositing their wet boots and coats, Izzy sniffed the air and said to her father: "I'm starving, and dinner smells good – what is it?"

"I would like to take credit for it," James said, directing his eyes toward Kate, "however, it's one of Lorna's chilli's," said James, with a dramatic air.

Izzy cheered, "Yeah! Oh, you'll love Lorna's chilli, Kate! She is a wonderful cook."

"You're right there, Izzy. Though I hope you like chilli, Kate."

Kate nodded vigorously and regretted it immediately, smiling instead, which was much less painful.

"Yes, I love chilli, and you make me feel even guiltier that I have not contributed anything to the meal."

"Today you are a guest, tomorrow I promise I will find you a little job to do, deal?"

"Deal," said Kate.

While Izzy laid the table, James put some garlic bread into the oven. Within minutes of them coming through the door from the freezing outdoors they were all sat down in the lovely warm and cozy kitchen. Kate sat quietly, taking in the banter between father and daughter whilst they served the meal. It was obvious to anyone that these two adored each other and had a special relationship, not only that of father and daughter but almost 'work-mates' and friends. The conversation was just general chatter about animals and tractors and getting food out to cows and how deep the snow was in the north field, but to an outsider, like Kate, it sounded heavenly, normal, happy, and uncomplicated.

Kate's mind had begun to accept that, for better or worse, and for the foreseeable future, she was going to be a guest in this home. She decided there and then to try her hardest to stop wallowing in self pity and start acting as grateful as she should be to this family. She knew that James and Izzy probably normally chatted over dinner about the farm, but she was also aware that they were trying to make Kate feel as though she needn't speak, or tell them anything, unless or until she felt she wanted to, and she loved them for it.

"Do you know, I think this really is the best chili I have ever tasted, who is Lorna? Did you say? Who cooked it for you?"

"Lorna and Keith are tenant farmers on Dad's land, and Lorna cooks for us, isn't that right Dad?"

"Yes, she is a fabulous cook and keeps our freezer filled for us. I can cook, but I'm afraid my range of meals is limited, so we have an arrangement with Lorna: she prepares them, and all we have to do is heat them up when we come in from work."

"Now that's what I call a good arrangement," Kate said.

The meal was a comfortable affair. James had opened a bottle of wine and Kate allowed herself one glass – James said it wouldn't do her any harm and would probably help her sleep. Kate laughed at that and said, "It doesn't seem to take much to make me sleep, judging by this morning. But you're right – if I have slept all day I may not sleep tonight, so a glass of wine would be nice, thank you. And, I promise tomorrow I will be a more useful part of your team, instead of a passenger."

Kate was beginning to feel that it was time, and only right, that she offered some kind of explanation for her sudden, and abrupt, appearance on their farm, and for their kindness toward a stranger without asking any questions. James seemed to sense this and steered the conversation toward Izzy's favorite subject – Christmas.

"I wonder what day it is tomorrow. I don't suppose you can remember, Kate, as you have had such a nasty blow on your head," James was saying, very tongue in cheek.

"Christmas Eve!" said Izzy, excitedly.

"Oh my, is it?" Kate could see that James was winding Izzy up, and she was playing along.

"Oh, Kate! Don't you just love Christmas?"

"Well, yes I do. But, and I must be honest, it is never quite the same when you grow up as it is when one is your age. How old are you anyway?"

"I'm seven, and so is Elsa. We have been friends ever since we were little together, haven't we, Dad."

"You sure have: a bundle of mischief and a bundle of fun. We'll let Kate choose which was which."

"Well, I am almost sure that Izzy was the … mischief?" said Kate.

"No, no! Grandpa Andy always says I was like a cherub."

And Kate thought, she could just imagine it, in fact that was a perfect description of her.

"So Izzy, what are you getting for Christmas?" asked Kate.

Izzy looked at Kate in a puzzled way, and said, "Erm, well I won't know until Christmas Day, will I?"

"Oh, erm, of course, how silly of me! Sorry, what I meant to say was: what have you on your wish list?" Kate retracted quickly, realizing that Izzy's Christmases were not like her own, where her father and mother just asked her what she wanted and then gave her the money to buy it, so that Christmas was a forgone conclusion.

"Oh no," said James, in a pained way. "You have opened up the flood gates, now." James face wore a look of agony. "Izzy wishes for everything from a calf being born on Christmas Eve – so that she can actually call it Rudolph – to snow falling on Christmas Eve, which we already have, so that's one we don't have to worry about, to me getting married and providing her with a sister or a brother." At which everyone laughed.

"Well," Izzy said gravely, "You know what Tiny Tim says: if I can't have none of them, I might as well wish for all of them. However, failing that," she said in a much lighter and more conspirital tone, "something for Muffin – she's my pony. If you're well enough tomorrow, I will show you Muffin. You will love her, won't she, Dad?"

"Yes, I'm sure she will. But I think it's time you went up to bed now, because, no doubt, you will not have a wink of sleep tomorrow night."

"You're right. Oh, I can't wait, it's too exciting, isn't it? And I'm so glad you will be spending Christmas with us, Kate."

"I am really glad that I am too, Izzy. And I am very grateful for all your kindness to me since I landed on you. And I can't wait to see Muffin in the morning, good night."

As Izzy bounced up the stairs to bed, Kate stood to clear the dishes, to which James said, "Don't worry, they all just go into the dishwasher. You go through and I will bring the coffee in."

When Kate hesitated, James insisted, "Go! You are still an invalid. Just because you're walking around, that does not mean you're better."

"Yes sir," said Kate, in a mock subservient manner.

Kate went into the living room and it was obvious that Izzy had been in and put the Christmas tree lights on, which twinkled in the darkened room. With only the glow from the fire, and the table lamps, it looked warm and cozy. As she sat down carefully on the sofa, something washed over Kate: a feeling of calm. She knew that she had big problems to sort out and that the desolate feelings of emptiness were still uppermost in her thoughts, but for now she seemed to have called a truce with her feelings, and she had come to terms with the fact that it was Christmas. Yes, she was stranded in a farm in the middle of nowhere, and her personal life was in tatters, she thought, but her emotions were on hold until this unreal situation played out, which no doubt would be after the Christmas holidays, when she would return to her own world. But in the meantime, Kate decided to take advantage of the breathing space and just enjoy this wonderful family's kindness and hospitality, and try to not spoil Christmas for them.

James came in carrying the coffee on a tray, and the remainder of the bottle of wine and two glasses.

"As you don't appear to have had any adverse reactions, from the first glass, I thought you might want another one before bed."
He sat down in the big, deep-buttoned, leather, Chesterfield chair. It would have looked ridiculously large with anyone else sitting in it,

but for some reason it looked just right for James' long lean frame.

James poured the coffee and opened up the doors on the log burner. He instructed Kate, gently, to put her feet up, and rest back against the cushions, before giving her a cup and saucer with wonderful smelling fresh coffee.

"You know, I do not know how to thank you for all of your kindness."

James started to brush off her words, but Kate stopped him:

"No, James." It still seemed strange to be so familiar with someone that essentially she did not know, yet for some reason, it seemed so right. "No. I think the time has come to try and explain to you what happened. Well, as much as I know, because I can't remember some of it, and I can only sort of piece it together by a process of guess work.

"My name is Kate Johnson, and I am from Manchester, as I have already told you, apparently. I work for a large firm as a financial director. Actually, that sounds too grand; I have a degree in business and finance. I am thirty-five years old and single, and my boyfriend, Dominic, also works in the city, and is a banker."

Kate's voice became softer, and she spoke in a sort of reminiscent way, as she began to think about her life in abstract.

"Dominic and I have been together almost three years.

We planned this holiday for months. We were going to ski in Inverurie," said Kate, imitating the Scottish accent. "It all sounded so Scottish and Christmassy when we booked it, in August: a log cabin, skiing down the slopes of pure white snow, snuggling up in the evenings with a glass of wine in front of a roaring fire. I still don't understand what happened, what went wrong. Everything was going as planned: we arrived and booked into the lodge. We were so lucky because the snow was really coming down, and if Dominic hadn't borrowed his friends four wheel drive, instead of bringing his own Porsche, we would never have made it. However, we did, and everything was fine.

"I thought everything was fine, but then he did get a phone call, which seemed to worry him a little, but that is perfectly normal in the banking and finance profession, there is no such thing as holiday.

"As we sat down in front of the roaring fire, it was just as I had imagined it would be, so I told him my exciting news, which I thought would be the cherry on top of the proverbial cake: that I was pregnant; only about two months, but enough to know, and to do a test which showed positive. I was thrilled, I couldn't wait to tell him when I found out, but I didn't. I bottled my excitement up because I wanted the moment to be just right."

James sat silently, though Kate probably wouldn't have noticed even if he had left the room. She was reliving the moment in utter clarity.

"Dominic was furious, he began shouting at me, telling me he just worked at the bank, he didn't own it. I thought he was just shocked and I tried to calm him down, and explained that I knew it was a shock and it had come out of the blue, but sometimes that's the best way. I explained that sometimes good things happen that way. You know how you babble on when you want someone to understand as you do.

"Then he got really, really nasty, and grabbed me by the chin. He shouted at me that he never wanted to see me, or 'my' baby, ever again.

"When I said to him, 'Dominic, you don't mean it, you are just shocked,' he lifted his hand and hit me across the face."

What seemed like a long silence hung between Kate and James, but he never spoke or tried to comfort her, somehow he knew that wasn't the end.

"I think I must have hit my head on the corner of the fire place. The next thing I knew, I found myself face down in the snow..." Kate's voice trailed away.

"I have never ever seen Dominic be violent, to anyone, in all the time we have been together. I have never seen that look on his face. It's a look which I will never, ever forget. The look was one of pure hatred.

"When I found myself in the snow, in one of my more lucid moments, I thought I must have had a car crash, because why else would I have been injured? It wasn't until I was in the bath, after you had found my suitcase and my handbag, that my mind was trying to make sense of it, and could start to figure it out. It was then that I opened my case, and in it I found my pregnancy test kit, which I had put in my box of tampons, ironically, to hide it, until the big surprise. Then it all came back to me: I had not had an accident, Dominic had hit me. Dominic had hit me so hard..." she said, with a sob beginning to force its way into her chest area, "...that I lost my baby. That precious, precious, new life, which was only just beginning to grow, and he killed it."

The tears were running down Kate's face, silently streaming, but the wracking sobs of before didn't come. They sat quietly. Neither one of them spoke until, in the blink of an eye, she was back with him.

"Well that's it. That's what my mind didn't want to remember, so I managed to blot it out for a while. But you can't hide forever, can you?"

James reached out and took one of Kate's hands in his, before saying, "You know, without me telling you that it was better you found out before you married him, or had children to him, men who have that kind of violence in them, well, eventually it will come out, sooner or later." James voice was soft, and as he spoke, he rubbed the back of her hand with his thumb in a soothing manner.

"Listen Kate, you need time to rest and recuperate. You need time to heal, not only from your injuries, but in your mind. Finding that the person you have been with for three years is not what you thought, and losing your baby, is not something you can put behind you easily. You are more than welcome to stay with Izzy and I. You are quite safe here, I promise you. You will just have to take my word on that, but you do have Elsa and Izzy to protect you,"
James said, trying to introduce a note of lightness into a very tense situation. "Sleep on it, Kate."

As James stood up from the arm chair, he knelt over Kate and lifted her legs onto the sofa, and covered her with the blanket. He put another log on the fire, and turned to switch the lamps off, when Kate asked if he wouldn't mind leaving the tree lights on, and as they seemed to give her comfort, he did.

As James walked towards the stairs, Kate said into the darkness, "Thank you, thank you, James."

The words didn't require any answer, they were said in such a way that James knew that Kate trusted him, that she knew that he understood her need to grieve and hide away from the world for a while, and that she would take him up on his offer of sanctuary.

Chapter 6

Kate slept soundly that night and woke up bright and early the next morning, having slept most of the previous day. It was before five and the house was still quiet. Even Elsa, her faithful watchdog, appeared to be out for the count, lying as close to the sofa as she could without actually being on it. Today, Kate thought to herself, she didn't want to be depressing, which would spoil what should be a happy and exciting day for Izzy. Yesterday Kate had still been in denial about the whole episode with Dominic, and how she had landed on this farm in the middle of nowhere.

Telling her story to James had had a cathartic effect on Kate. Simply talking about it step by step made it clear in her mind. James hadn't even said a word, he had simply listened while she spilled the whole sad story out. Kate decided there and then that she would make the supreme effort to put her sadness aside until she was able to get back to her life and sort things out with Dominic. It served no purpose to make these kind people miserable, and she certainly did not intend to spoil their Christmas.

Although she was in a lot of pain from her ribs, the pain in her head had subsided, and if she didn't look in the mirror she could almost forget that she looked like Quasimodo, with a huge black, blue, and yellow swelling on her eye, which by now she could open slightly, to her relief. Kate got up, trying not to wake Elsa, but as soon as she moved, Elsa seemed to have some sort of inbuilt radar, and was up on protection duty. Kate battled with the blanket, attempting to fold it while Elsa was trying to lick her to death. She opened the fire doors and put on some logs to make sure the lounge was warm for when James and Izzy came down.

She decided to have her shower early. Today was the day she was determined to 'do her bit', and in doing so, maybe it would help lift her spirits at the same time, after all it was Christmas Eve, even if it didn't feel like it. Remembering what James had said, about how the shower worked, Kate let the water run until it was piping hot then stood underneath it, soothing her aching body. She felt a bit like an Egyptian mummy, unravelling the strapping which James had put on to hold her ribs together, and it also felt lovely to get it all off.

Kate struggled with her hair at first, trying to keep it out of the water because of the dressing, which she could feel with her probing fingers. But, after awhile, the temptation to put her head under the streaming hot liquid was too much, and she decided that she would worry about the dressing when she was finished.

It was heaven. She found all the toiletries she needed and soaped her whole body, washed her blood matted hair, then very gently washed her very tender face.

The very action of having a shower made Kate feel ready to start the day afresh: her thoughts were now more in order. She ticked off the positives in her mind: I know what happened; I know why it happened … well sort of; I know where I am, sort of; I am safe; she said to herself with absolute conviction. I am lucky to be alive, she said to herself as a final thought on the subject before turning the water off and getting out of the shower.

Kate managed to dress herself, even managing to put the strapping back on in a kind of fashion – it wasn't very tight but it was on. Pulling her jeans over her very slim figure was an achievement in itself, as it was the first time she had been able to dress herself since she arrived. Pulling her sweater gingerly over her head, she wrapped a towel around her hair. Forgetting about the bathroom mirror, Kate caught sight of her reflection, just as she had done yesterday. However, today she was not as shocked, she knew now that whatever it was, making her face so tender, would not look very good, but at least she could see out of her eye a little better. Kate felt almost ready to start the day: she felt stronger, not only in body but in a deep breath sort of way, as though she had taken a weight off her shoulders, which she presumed was because she had shared her problem with James – you know what they say: a trouble shared is a trouble halved, or something like that.

Kate wandered around the wonderfully warm kitchen, and for the first time, she actually saw the room. For the last two days she had been in a dream and could have been anywhere. Oh, she remembered being warm and the smell being wholesome, but she had not taken in her surroundings. She loved it; it was like something on an 'escape to the country' programme off the television. Not at all like what she herself was used too: her little one bedroom apartment with its en suite, which was almost a cupboard. Oh, yes – she had a lovely lounge and a kitchen, and it cost a fortune in the Centre of Manchester; it had once been an old Warehouse, which had been converted to very expensive trendy apartments. To its detriment, it was functional rather than homely, and practical rather than cozy. Oh, but this, she thought, was a whole different ball game.

In one corner of the kitchen was, what estate agents would call, a 'bonket', where the table was set into a corner and the seating went round the back of the table and it had a selection of wooden chairs at the front of it. The Aga, of course, which was what was keeping the whole place so toasty warm. It did not have posh kitchen units, actually the cupboards and welsh dresser almost looked home made, and were all individual, but somehow they looked wonderful in this perfect setting. The floor was stone flags with the odd rush mat strewn over them, highly suitable for dirty feet and dogs muddy paws.

After examining the kitchen, Kate started to hunt for the utensils, plates, and cups. She thought: I may not be able to cook for James and Izzy, but I could at least lay the table. She presumed they had lots of work on today, with it being Christmas Eve, though really she had no idea what, as she had never been on a farm in her life, but she was sure it was a busy day.

As Kate was filling the kettle and was about to find out where on earth it went on the massive Aga, a movement behind her made her turn quickly, making her wince.

"Oh, I'm sorry. I didn't mean to give you a fright, it's a nice surprise having someone up before me in the morning. I usually crawl down in the dark and don't even bother with coffee until I have fed the stock."

"Hi," said Kate, feeling a little shy this morning, not only for being caught rummaging around James' kitchen, but after bearing her soul to him the night before, she didn't really know how to cope with the first meeting with him.

"Shall I leave the coffee until you come back in then?" Kate said, a little uncertain of her ground.

"No, no, coffee would be great. To be honest, when you live on your own, like Izzy and I do, you forget the niceties of life and just get into a routine of work, eat, and sleep."

"Oh, I don't think that can be true, you and Izzy appear, from what I've seen so far, to have a wonderful life."

"Oh, your right, don't get me wrong, it's the best life in the world. And nobody forced me into farming, I chose it and I love everything about it. No, I suppose what I meant was, when you don't have a woman about the place, you tend to let things drop that a normal family would do, such as a family breakfast."

"I was trying to work out where the kettle goes on this … 'Cooker'?" Kate said.

James laughed and went to lift the lid on the Aga to show Kate how simple it was. As he lifted one of the four lids on the double size Aga, the heat from the plate warmed Kate's face, and she stepped back in surprise backing into James.

"Oops, sorry! Wow, that's instant heat! How wonderful is that? How on earth do you control the heat? Is that on all the time then? You didn't have to switch it on like a normal cooker?"

James laughed at the barrage of questions from an obvious city girl.

"Your welcome," said James, as he placed his hands on Kate's shoulders from behind, where she had stepped into him. "Yes, they are great. They are very easy to control once you are used to them, and yes, it's on all the time."

James laughed again, saying, "It's well to be seen you have never been on a farm before. Having said that, I would be lying to you if I didn't confess that I have a foot in both camps. I am neither a city boy nor a born and bred farmer. I am an imposter."

At Kate's look of puzzlement, James clarified: "My parents owned this farm, and although I did grow up most of the time here, in actual fact we belonged in Edinburgh. My parents are both solicitors and this was supposed to be their country idyll. However, they soon realized, when you buy a country estate you have responsibilities to the land and the tenants who live off it.

"So if you are not a born and bred farmer, what are you?"
Kate asked, intrigued to know how a man who looked more suited to the land than she could ever have imagined had ended up here.

"I am a journalist. Well, I was journalist – a foreign journalist, mostly free lance, working in the Middle East and Asia. But I gave it up to become a farmer when my parents were too old and my father became ill. They are happier in their Edinburgh apartment now, and I am much happier being a farmer, so it all worked out for the best."

Kate suddenly noticed the kettle, which had been boiling away. She reached to take it off the hob and James said quickly,
"Ah, ah," giving Kate the oven mitt.

"You will soon learn that everything on the Aga is hot, especially pan handles. You will, of course, burn yourself, before it becomes indelibly printed in your head, to always use the oven mitt."

James showed Kate where the mugs and the coffee were kept so she would know the next time, and they were soon sitting down at the kitchen table. Kate said she felt so much better today despite what she knew she must look like, and that she really wanted to help and not be a hindrance, when she knew they must have a lot of things to do, it being Christmas Eve and all.

James laughed and said to Kate: "I think you're under the impression that we are a dairy farm, or turkey farmers. No, today is no different from any other day for us: we still have stock to feed and the normal routine of the farm, but we don't have to meet a Christmas deadline for the retail trade. We have cows with calves to feed in the barns, Silage to drop in the fields, horses to feed and muck out, and Izzy has her chickens, and there are always jobs to be done, but even I relax and enjoy Christmas. The weather is set to get worse. I'm afraid, so I am really pleased you feel a little better, you had me worried there. I was panicking about getting you to Aberdeen for an X ray on those ribs."

"Oh, I had a shower and managed to put the strapping back on. It's probably not as tight as it should be, but they feel a lot less painful," Kate said with a slight blush, realizing he would probably offer to re-do it, and for some reason, once you are on the mend and have your wits about you, it becomes more embarrassing.

"I have probably dislodged the plaster you put on my head, but once I was under the lovely hot water, I couldn't resist washing my hair. And as for the eye, well, what can I say, I get a fright every time I see myself in the bathroom mirror."

They both laughed and agreed it was a bit of a mess.

"Izzy thought you were very pretty, despite your eye."

And they laughed again as James tried to take his foot out of his mouth, saying he also thought she was pretty despite the eye.

"If you would really like a job while Izzy and I are busy … speaking of Izzy, where on earth is she this morning?"

As if by magic, Izzy came bounding into the kitchen.

"Why didn't you wake me up Dad? I want to enjoy the whole day, it's…?"

"Christmas Eve!" they all said in unison, and then they all laughed together, just like a proper family, thought Izzy.

"If you would both like to set the table, we might all sit down and have a proper breakfast this morning. Just give me an hour to do the cows. Kate might want to come and watch us do the horses after breakfast, Izzy, if she feels okay."

James looked at Kate enquiringly.

"Oh, yes, that would be smashing! And I can show you Muffin, Kate. You will love her!" Izzy said, with barely concealed excitement bubbling up inside her, and shining out of her lovely little face.

Having Kate to stay for Christmas, showing her Muffin, Christmas Eve tonight, it couldn't get any better than that, thought Izzy.

Kate thought, how lovely to be Izzy's age, with no worries, and on Christmas Eve. How wonderful life was when you were young and innocent. While Izzy and Kate were laying the table, Kate, unused to chatting with children, and not sure what made them tick, even at seven in the morning, embarked on a subject which she knew was close to Izzy's heart.

"So what's the routine on Christmas day, Izzy? How do you and your dad normally spend Christmas?"

"Oh well, normally Grandpa Andy and Grandma Ailsa come from Edinburgh and they usually stay for two weeks. They do the cooking, Grandma is a lovely cook, she brings all kinds of goodies, and Grandpa Andy is chief-washer-upper, he says. Dad gives any cows that are in the barn extra feed the night before, and the horses have extra feed so that in the morning, when we get up, we can open our presents before he goes out."

Izzy's face was aglow with unconcealed excitement. "I normally have all my presents in front of the fire, on the sofa. And Dad, Grandpa and Grandma's presents are under the Christmas tree."

"Oh well, I better find somewhere else to sleep, or Santa Claus won't be able to lay your presents out, will he?"

"Oh no, I didn't mean that! But you could always sleep in Grandpa and Grandma's room, it's lovely and it was all ready for them until grandpa took ill. Grandpa says Grandma is fussing, but he must really be ill, or he would not have stayed in bed as long as he has, Dad says. Dad says Grandpa has something wrong with his chest or something and, with the weather and all, they have to stay in Edinburgh, and it will be the very first year that they have not been here with us since I was a baby, so I'm really glad you are going to be here, Kate."

James came into the kitchen after leaving his wet things in the boot room. His cheeks were rosy and he smelled of fresh air.

"So what have you two been chatting about? Or shall I try and guess?"

"Christmas!" they all chimed.

"Actually, that was my doing; I was asking Izzy all about the Christmas routine, which involves me sleeping on her special place, the sofa," Kate said.

"Dad, Kate could sleep in Grandma and Grandpa's room, couldn't she? Now that she is a little better and can climb the stairs?"

"I don't mean to intrude and I don't mind where you put me, but, Izzy tells me, Santa

Claus usually leaves her presents on the sofa in front of the fire, and I don't think he would do that if I were sleeping there," Kate said with a straight face, but a smile in her eye, which James definitely spotted.

"Oh, you're right of course," James said in an exaggerated way. "I never gave it a thought, I'm sure you would be more comfortable in my parent's room anyway. It's just as well they didn't attempt to come this year, who would have guessed how much snow we would get before Christmas? We are used to the snow, but the way my parents are, you know, at their age, and Dad's not well, the Doctor's told him it's pleurisy, and he must be poorly, because normally you could not have kept him in bed unless he was nailed to it. And though my mum tells me he is complaining, he is still not strong enough to get up, by all accounts. So it's just us two this year, or was … now it's us three."

Breakfast was a happy and relaxed meal. They chatted and planned the day ahead and Kate listened with pleasure.

"First things first, we need to put a new dressing on your head and then you can dry your hair properly, and I better tighten the strapping on your ribs, it's important for it to be tight to help support them."

It was agreed that, if Kate was well enough, she could walk to the barn for a little fresh air and see the horses, but that was all, James said in a firm tone. Kate would wear Grandma's wellingtons, as the snow was so deep it would have gone over her ski boots, and she certainly could not have laced them up, as she still could not bend.

Kate felt less embarrassed, strangely enough, when James strapped her ribs this time. After all, she reasoned, she did have her bra on, and it was obvious that he did this in a very clinical way, as though he were strapping a horse or a cow, she told herself. James put a new dressing on her head after inspecting his handy work, telling Kate with relief that it looked an awful lot better than it did two days ago, in fact the swelling had gone down a little and the cut had begun to knit together. Kate managed to dry her hair with Izzy's hair dryer, staying well away from the sore area, which to her seemed to be right across the top of her head. By the time that

that was done, Izzy had loaded the dish washer, and had put Grandma's wellingtons, and long waterproof coat, ready for Kate to wear.

"Do you know you have a *treasure* for a daughter? If I had a little girl I would want her to be like you, Izzy," Kate said, and suddenly she had a lump in her throat, as she realized what she had said about having a little girl.

James noticed, and immediately, to ease the tension, said, "Oh, she has her moments. Right, let's get to work."

He helped Kate on with her wellies and coat, asking if she was sure, as just walking to the barn would jolt her ribs, but Kate was adamant she wanted to try.

As they opened the outside door from the boot room, James said, "Your chariot awaits, my lady."

Izzy hooted with laughter, as outside the door was the quad bike, with a box hitched to the back of it. This was normally used to transport sheep with lambs, or the dogs or hay, or anything really, that needed to be transported around the farm.

Kate took one look and said, "Is it safe?

"What this? Yes, yes of course. This little beauty carries everything and anything and can certainly carry a little thing like you to the barn. Come on, it's better than you struggling through the deep snow before your ribs have even had a chance to heal."

Well, Kate decided, she was game for anything. Izzy held her arm as she climbed into the box, James put the tailgate up and got onto the quad.

"Hang on tight now".

Kate held the edge of the trailer, but James said for her to hang on tight to his shoulders, so she gripped his shoulders and could feel his solid form beneath his coat. And off they went. Izzy ran beside it as best she could, but the snow was even deeper than last night, and her little legs were sinking right down into the freshly fallen snow. The snow clouds above, still ominously full, had parted temporarily, which allowed a bright shaft of watery sun to slip through the gap, but it was obvious that there was a lot more snow to come before nightfall.

Tip and Elsa appeared, from one of the barns, and obviously thought this was a game and came running through the snow. They barked at the quad bike with James and Kate in the box. James shouted to Kate, "Don't worry if Tip jumps in the trailer, he won't harm you. He thinks I'm going somewhere, and he would usually come, too."

Luckily, they were at the barn by this time. It was not that Kate was afraid of dogs, but she didn't want Tip to think she had taken his place, she had only ever seen collies on *One Man And His Dog* on television, but she knew they could be territorial.

Chapter 7

The barn door had been opened so that James could ride the quad and the trailer straight inside, closely followed by the barking dogs and Izzy struggling to keep up behind them all, and she was thoroughly puffed out and pink cheeked.

Kate gasped at the sheer size of the barn and tried to imagine anything she had ever seen which was as massive as this. The only thing she could think of was when she had gone to a rock concert, which was being held at an old aerodrome hanger. All down one side in separated stalls was where the farm machinery was kept in the winter. On the same side as the machinery were stalls full of hay and silage bales, which were stacked to the roof. On the other side were stalls for the horses, although it looked as though they had enough room for a dozen horses, it looked as though only four of the stalls were in use.

James stopped the quad and came round to help Kate out of the trailer. Izzy came puffing and panting in behind them with the dogs almost knocking her over in their hurry to be where all the action was. The first thing that Kate noticed, apart from the sheer size of the barn, was the noise. Not from this barn, but she assumed the loud mooing noises were coming from the other barns. She had never heard a cow close up; in fact she didn't really think she had ever really noticed a cow in a field being unusually noisy, so she was totally unprepared for the unholy racket that seemed to rattle around the tin roofs of the barns. James, Izzy, and the dogs didn't seem to even notice, whereas Kate's face was a picture, and James suddenly realized that this 'townie' was in farm-shock, and he laughed, saying to Izzy in a loud voice, "This is a quiet day, isn't it Izzy?"

"Most of the herd is out in the fields, I only bring them in to calve, then I keep them in for a while until the calf is strong enough to withstand the weather. October Calves often stay in a bit longer because of the harsh conditions up here. You get used to the noise so you don't even notice it after a while." Kate doubted this but tried her best to concentrate.

"Come on Kate, come and meet Muffin, you will love her. She is 10 years old and she is 12 hands. And isn't she the most beautiful colour you have ever seen? She is a Dapple Grey Welsh. Isn't she just the best horse you have ever seen in your life?" Izzy said, bursting with pride and affection for her pony.

"Well, actually Izzy, she is the first and only horse I have ever seen in my life – well, close up that is. I mean, I have seen them in fields, but to be honest I have never been this close to a live … thing … as big as this. But, oh, you are so right, she is absolutely beautiful! Wow, what lovely long eye lashes she has, and what a gorgeous colour."

Kate tentatively moved forward and looked to Izzy, to see if it was safe to stroke her. Izzy nodded vigorously, saying that the horse would love it and that she really was a sweetie and was as gentle as a lamb.

"Here Kate, give her a carrot. You will be her friend forever. She loves carrots, but hold it in the flat of your hand. Yes, that's it. And don't get a fright when she licks it off."

Izzy laughed at Kate's nervous expression and the wincing look on her face. Kate was really intrigued with the gentleness of the horse's mouth as it took the carrot from her open hand. Feeling a little bolder, Kate patted the side of Muffin's neck, just like Izzy did. Muffin turned her head to see who this stranger was, but seemed quite happy to let her pat her.

"Izzy, you're right, she is lovely, but isn't she a little large for you to ride, as you are so young," Kate glanced at James, who was standing and watching Kate and Izzy together.

"Izzy has ridden since she was about three years old, with my guidance, of course. She is a very competent rider and can more than handle Muffin; In fact, she often takes Merlin out – Muffin's mother, who is even larger, at 15 hands – just to give her a little gentle exercise. She's very old now, she must be 25 year old, isn't that right Izzy?"

Izzy nodded and added, "But she is so gentle, even a beginner could sit on Merlin and be completely safe," with a smile on her face while looking at her father and glancing at Kate, and they both laughed. Kate was so absorbed in how still Muffin was standing and letting Kate pat her that she didn't notice the exchange. "Come and see Dad's horses Kate. If you think Muffin is big, wait until you see Glen."

They passed the stall after Muffin's, which had Merlin in it, who was also dapple like her daughter. Then the next stall had the most enormous horse Kate thought she might ever see in her life.

"This is Glen," said James. "Well, actually his real name is Glenmore, and he is my horse, well one of my horses, but I am the only one who rides him. He is a very well behaved horse but he is strong and is only used to having me on his back."

"He is enormous," Kate repeated. "How tall is he?" she asked in a naive sort of way.

"Well, you measure a horse by hands, and he is about sixteen and a half hands, which actually is not as tall as some show horses, which can be eighteen hands, yet they are still agile enough to jump."

"He is absolutely beautiful, but I think I will stay on this side of the stall, if you don't mind." James patted Glen and told him it was nothing personal, but after all she is a townie, he whispered into Glen's ear in a sort of stage whisper.

The next stall had a beautiful Mare, which James called Midnight. She was a Dutch warm blood who was eighteen years old, James told Kate, and it was obvious where her name had come from – she was the most midnight black and blue you could ever imagine. As they came to the next stall the horse's head that leaned over towards Kate was the most gorgeous thing Kate had ever seen. The name plate on the front of the stall said Sapphire, and her name fitted her perfectly. James explained that Sapphire was Midnight's filly, now nine years old.

Kate was immediately struck by Sapphire. She took an instant liking to this horse, even though it seemed tall. For some reason Kate wasn't afraid.

"Oh, she's beautiful! She is the most beautiful thing I have ever seen."

Kate patted Sapphires neck and went to reach for a carrot out of the sack. She looked at both Izzy and James to see if it would be all right to give it to her. James said of course, and could see that Kate had made an instant connection with Sapphire, which was ironic as the horse had always been meant for Jenny, his wife, but she never rode it. James had brought the horse on as a young filly, with the idea that Jenny would have her when she was old enough to be ridden.

"Would you like to stroke her Kate? She is a lovely natured horse and won't hurt you."

"Oh yes, I would love to! She is gorgeous."

James opened the stall and told Sapphire calmly that they had come to say hello and that she must be a good girl. As he spoke to the horse he ran his hand gently over her back. Sapphire didn't move, she just blew out of her nostrils, and for some reason that Kate could not explain, she didn't feel frightened. Kate felt as though the horse knew that she was nervous and inexperienced, and stood very quietly so as to not frighten Kate. It was the most wonderful experience of Kate's life – from that moment on Kate was totally smitten; she had never had a pet and didn't know anything about animals, really, but in that instant she knew how those who work with them everyday could gain pleasure out of doing so.

Kate stroked the horse's neck and it felt warm beneath her touch. Sapphire slowly turned her head toward Kate and put her mouth gently towards Kate's face. James told her, in a lowered voice, that Sapphire was simply smelling her and seeing who she was, and that Kate needn't be afraid.

Kate wasn't afraid. She lifted her hand and stroked Sapphire's nose and cheek, and as she stroked, she gained in confidence, and totally enjoyed the whole experience. They stepped slowly back from Sapphire, and out of the stall, and Kate's face was radiant. For someone who had never been up close and personal with anything larger than a kitten, she was amazed at her seemingly natural comfort.

"How wonderful! Now I see why you love your Muffin, Izzy. It's catching, I think."

"Come on Kate, I want to show you my chickens."

Izzy caught hold of Kate's hand and James intervened, saying, "Slowly Izzy, give Kate a chance. She is not properly healed. You know this is her first time out, so don't wear her out."

But that was said with a smile to his daughter so that she knew he wasn't chastising her.

The bottom stall in the barn was split into two completely separate chicken runs, each with its own little hen house. They sort of looked like large dolls houses with the front taken off, and inside there were separate little shelves with straw on them. Izzy explained that she had two different types of chickens, and to keep them pure bred they must have completely different chicken houses and runs. The little houses with the shelves in were where the hens laid their eggs had to be separate too.

"I intend to breed and sell the young in the future, so they must stay pure bred, which means they must not get into each others' runs," said Izzy, with great authority in her voice. It was clear she knew exactly what she was talking about and took her chickens very seriously.

"Izzy, you are a marvel. I am sure at seven years old I didn't even know where eggs came from; I probably thought they came from the supermarket."

They all laughed at Kate's admission. In fact, she also told them she had never even been to a petting farm, so she had never been as close as this to any farm animals in her life. And then she said to both of them, "And do you know what? I have sadly missed out on my education, and I intend to do something about that in future."

The future Kate spoke of was vague, and best left that way for now. Her stay here was inevitable, for several reasons, but she was determined she would not be unhappy. She was going to take this time to experience knew things – every new thing that came her way, she would embrace it. If the last week had taught her anything at all, it was that nothing was certain and nothing was set in concrete – there was always time to change the future.

The weather was closing in when they left the barn to come back to the house. Snow had begun to fall again quite heavily and there was a definite chill in the air. As they came into the boot room, Elsa shook her wet fur, and Izzy and Kate screamed while James just laughed. Kate sat down on the old wooden bench, which was designed for sitting on while putting on or taking off your boots. Kate sat while Izzy pulled her boots off for her.

"Thank you, Izzy. I have really enjoyed you showing all your animals to me, and thank you for helping me with my boots."

"Oh, you're welcome! It's lovely to have another girl here to talk to."

"Ha, a girl! Oh Izzy, you are priceless, it's a long time since I've been called a girl, but I wish I'd had you for a sister when I was little, I would have loved it."

Once they had all dumped their coats and boots, they went into the lovely warm kitchen where James was looking over a large box on the kitchen table.

"What is it Dad? Is it something for Christmas? Is it a surprise?"

"Well, yes, it is for Christmas. And it is a surprise."

James was reading a note which he had found taped to the lid of the box.

"It's from Lorna and Keith, they must have called while we were in the barn. They were in a hurry, the note says, because the jeep was acting up. They heard that grandma and grandpa are not coming this year, and they say we are invited to come to them, but they know we wouldn't leave the house on Christmas day, so they have left us," James peered into the box.

"What does it look like, Christmas Dinner?"

James looked again in the box and started to lift out various pie dishes, laying them on the table as he looked into each one, saying aloud, "Mashed potatoes, roast potatoes, parsnips, carrots and sprouts. And for the *piece de resistance*, one of Lorna's turkeys. Can you believe that woman?" James said, absently, "they can not afford to do this for us, but it's typical of them both. Well you should both be very grateful, as it saves you both from a fate worse than death. Because ..." he said with dramatic pause, "I was going to cook for us!" James said with a hideous laugh.

"How very kind of her," said Kate. "Is she your neighbour?
Ah, yes. Izzy told me. She cooks for you and fills your freezer, but you seem to live in the middle of nowhere, from what I have seen in the

brief time I've been here. She was brave to come out in this weather."

"Yes, Lorna is one of the tenant farmers who live on our land. Lorna and Keith, and Morag and Eaden both farm five hundred acres of Comraich land. You're right, the weather is pretty bad, and that old jeep of theirs is always breaking down. I will just go and give her a ring to thank her for her usual thoughtfulness and to make sure she got home all right."

James was back within minutes.

"The lines are down. I'm not surprised, mind, it happens every year. One of these days I will have to have the lines put underground. The only reason I haven't so far is the huge cost involved. It's not simply a cable, it has to be taken to the nearest main cable, which is miles away, and the cost of laying it will be astronomical."

"How will you know if they got home or not?" Kate said in a worried tone, with concern for the very kind couple who had just delivered Christmas in a box in spite of the risk to themselves."

"Oh, don't worry. We have a shortwave. I will give it an hour and then see if they're back home. They would probably not be in the house at the moment anyway, I suppose, when I think about it. They are turkey farmers, so they will be busy. People will be arriving to collect their turkeys for most of the day."

Izzy piped up, "It's a good job, she got rid of most of them at the farmer's market the other day, Dad",

"You're right, Izzy, normal folk don't like to attempt to come up this far in weather like this, even for their turkey."

"A shortwave?" Kate asked. "Is that some sort of short range telephone?"

"Well, you could say that it's a short wave radio, but actually you can pick up all kinds of distances, if the skip is right – the radio waves…" he said, to clarify what skip was.

"Ah, so you're not totally cut off then."

"Well, we only mainly use it to talk to Lorna and Morag, as the telephone wires have been down often in bad weather conditions, so we have all found it beneficial to have the shortwave.

"Listen, you need to rest now. I think you have done far too much for one day. I need to go back into the barns for a couple of hours, so before I go I will show you your bedroom, erm, my parents bedroom, and you could have a little rest before we eat, okay?"

James walked in front of Kate up the stairs and showed her into a large double bedroom along the landing. It had a large, old-fashioned, metal frame bed, with brass knobs on each post. The bed was covered with a beautiful home made patchwork quilt, which looked so sumptuous that you could sink right into it and sleep like a log, thought Kate. There was a scrubbed pine dressing table on one wall, and little pine cabinets on either side of the bed with a table lamp on each. The dormer window was dressed with little curtains that looked to have been hand made by the same person who had obviously made the beautiful quilt – James' mother, Kate presumed, or maybe not, maybe his ex-wife, who knows?

James had already carried Kate's suitcase upstairs for her and put it in the room.

"If there is anything you need, just shout, and Izzy will be about. But please make yourself at home. I will be in as soon as I'm finished in the barn, okay?"

Kate thanked James, shyly saying, "Please don't worry about me, you have done more than enough already. You must be a very busy man, and I feel as though I am taking up your valuable time. As if you didn't have enough to do without me making things worse. I'm sorry James…" said Kate, with a slight tremor in her voice, "if it wasn't for the weather, I would go, and leave you and Izzy to enjoy your Christmas in peace."

"Now, listen here…" said James, taking Kate by the hand, and sitting her down on the lovely soft bed. "You are not putting us to any trouble. We are really pleased to have you here, even if your arrival was a little unorthodox," he said with a smile in his voice. "You are more than welcome. And honestly, If Izzy could get any more excited, she would burst. She is really enjoying having another woman in the house, other than my mother, of course. And I have not had another woman in the house … other than my mother, of course, for a very long time, so I'm enjoying it too. So no more talk of being in the way. We'll think of this as a special Christmas for all of us when we look back. It may not be what you expected when you left Manchester, but maybe that was not meant to be. Okay?"

"Okay," said Kate, swallowing the lump which had formed in her throat because of the kind way James had spoken to her. *Her* – a complete stranger, who he had taken into his home. And with that thought, James left to go downstairs, and Kate lay on top of the bed with a soft wool blanket over. She only intended to rest her eyes and think about what James had said about not being what she had planned when she left Manchester; however, sleep must have overtaken her within seconds, and she slept the sleep of the contented and warm.

Chapter 8

When Kate woke up it was dusk and the clouds, which had threatened earlier, had now opened and were releasing another deluge of snow onto the already snow laden ground. She felt much better after her nap, and was able to roll off the bed without wincing, which was a huge step forward. Finding her way to the upstairs bathroom, Kate looked in the mirror and grimaced, but decided she must try and do something with her face and hair. She realized that she must be feeling better, as for the last three days, she did not care how James saw her, yet for some reason she wanted to try and make herself look more presentable.

After running a comb through her hair, whilst trying to avoid the still very sore part on her head, Kate then brushed her teeth. After rooting around in her make up bag, which consisted of very little, as Kate really didn't need make-up so she didn't buy it, she found a tube of concealer, which she occasionally used for the odd blemish. She dabbed at her black and blue eye very gingerly and then gently smoothed over the concealer, in an attempt to hide the worst of the discoloration. By now the swelling had gone down considerably so that Kate's features could clearly be seen once again. Kate stared at her reflection absently, not really seeing what was in front of her as her mind drifted back to when she was dressing for Dominic. She tried to remember the last time she had been really excited or ecstatically happy with him, and the only time in the recent past was when she found out she was pregnant. The sudden realization made her snap back from the past and she could see her reflection clearly now. Her jet black eyes were now brimming with tears, because it had become crystal clear to her in that flash back that she had hoped the baby would once again make her and Dominic happy.

Knowing that to be the truth, Kate realized that it would have been wrong to bring a new life into the world and hope it could paper over the cracks in a crumbling relationship. Somehow this had a cathartic affect on her, she swallowed hard and wiped away the tears, determined that she would enter into the spirit of Christmas if not for herself but for James and Izzy. One last look in the mirror and Kate decided it was the best she could do, and actually there had been a big improvement over the last three days.

Kate went down the stairs. Through the banisters she could see that the living room looked different from when she had gone to bed: the lamps were lit and the fire burned bright with fresh logs. The tree lights were glowing in the corner, and underneath the tree were some very interesting packages, which had not been there when she went up to bed. She could also smell what she hoped was another one of Lorna's wonderful dishes, as Kate suddenly realized her appetite had returned. At that moment her tummy gave a distinct rumble.

Walking into the kitchen and looking out of the window, she could see the barn lights were still on, which probably meant that James and Izzy were still working in there. Kate thought she would look in the oven and see if there was anything to be done to help dinner. She found the oven mitt and she remembered what James had said about burning herself before she learned the lesson. Lifting the lid off the casserole dish, Kate could distinguish that it was indeed some sort of wonderful smelling casserole. Seeing nothing else on the work tops, Kate decided to root around and see what she should make to go with it. In the boot room there was a long rack which held potatoes and vegetables, so she decided that, to save time, she would peel and cook some. Surely they would not come in wrong, and it was obvious that something must accompany the casserole.

Kate peeled the potatoes and vegetables, reaching up to the rack which hung above the units holding the heavy duty pans, the kind of pans that looked as though they could withstand the fierce heat from the Aga hotplates. She made the momentous decision to put the pans half on and half off the plate to heat, not knowing of any other way to measure the time for cooking on this monster of a cooker. The Aga was completely unlike her microwave, which was the only method of cooking she had in her apartment. Kate then laid the table, and by this time she was absolutely boiling in her thick polo sweater, which she was fed up of seeing herself in. With this in mind, she decided to nip upstairs and change into something smarter and cooler, after she checked that nothing would boil over on the Aga.

Whilst upstairs, Kate decided once and for all that she would be staying until the snow was passable, so she decided to put some clothes in the chest of draws. She quickly changed her sweater for a thin, stretch-round neck-top, of cream, with long sleeves. Over that she put a dark red, cropped, body warmer, and flicked her hair once again, which had the effect of spreading her dark, thick curls, over her shoulder, then she hurried downstairs.

To her relief, nothing had boiled over, and at that moment the back door burst open with the usual noise of boots being kicked free of snow, dogs barking, and excited voices. This time, as James and Izzy walked in the room, they didn't see a sad and distressed figure. James' eyes took in the sight of a completely different person, who actually had a lovely smile on her face, which was a greeting he very rarely got when he came in from the farm.

"Well, hello you … you look so much better. Doesn't she, Izzy?"

"Oh Kate, you do look better! You haven't got that big fat eye, which made you look like a freak…"

"Erm, well, thank you, Izzy – I think."

They all laughed, as it was obvious what Izzy had meant to say. Izzy was a wonderful child and didn't take offence as some would have and gone all shy. She just laughed with both James and Kate, then said quite earnestly, "No, I mean you look lovely … pretty now, doesn't she Dad? Didn't I say she would be pretty when her eye got better?"

"You did, Izzy. You saw her beauty even when she looked terrible, all covered in blood. Well, you should have an afternoon nap more often, if it does this for you."

"I hope you don't mind or have something different planned; I have cooked the potatoes and vegetables. I just guessed that that's what you would have with, what I presume, is one of Lorna's fabulous casseroles. And … erm, I'm not sure how to cook on that monster of a cooker. I couldn't find any knobs to turn the heat up or down, so I kind of hedged my bets and put them half on and half off, if that's okay."

"My my, you have been busy. That's great. We would have got round to that when we got in, but it is so nice to have dinner made for us for a change. We took longer in the barn than normal as we had a few things to do. Didn't we, Izzy?" said James with a wink.

"We gave the horses some extra feed. Didn't we, Dad?"

"Well, you did. Muffin will be as fat as butter if you're not careful. Anyway, this all looks very nice, and I give you full marks for battling with the Aga; it must be very strange for someone who has never lived in the country."

Kate's cheeks flushed, and a feeling of warmth spread through her like warm treacle, which had nothing to do with the heat of the kitchen. She had caught the bit that James said about her beauty, even when she was covered in blood. The compliments from both of them made Kate feel human again, and two inches taller, which was just what she needed at this time, even if they were said simply to cheer her up, they had done the trick.

"Okay, are we going to eat now? I'm starving." James said, and everyone sat down.

James insisted that Kate had done enough for one day and that he would serve the supper. Izzy excused herself for a moment, saying excitedly, "I'll be back in a second." She ran off and into the lounge, and within a few moments, the soft strains of Christmas music could be heard. Izzy came back and sat between her dad and Kate, and Kate could see that Izzy was really, really happy. It wasn't simply Christmas, though that had a lot to do with it, but she wondered if this little girl yearned for a family life with not only her favorite person in the world, her father, but also a mother, too. James had said that on Izzy's wish list was that he would get married and give Izzy a sister or a brother, so Kate thought she was obviously enjoying this little fantasy.

Kate would always remember this meal: they sat in the lovely, warm, homey kitchen; chatting together, and for the first time, she felt well enough to be part of the conversation, and not on the outside looking in. The talk was not of anything important, nor was it rocket science, it was just 'stuff': the weather, calves in the barn, Muffin – Izzy could always tell a tale about her horse and her chickens. James and Izzy had done most of tomorrow's jobs so that they could have a lazy day. They talked about Christmases of the past, when grandma and grandpa would normally be there, and what their traditions were. It was obvious to Kate that his parents were not just grandparents but were surrogate parents to Izzy, and by all accounts they must be lovely people, because they had raised a lovely son and grandchild.

Eventually, after the dishes had been cleared away, they all moved into the lounge to sit in front of the log burner. James brought in coffee for himself and Kate and chocolate for Izzy. Kate and Izzy were lounging on the sofa and James took his usual chair. The only lights on in the room were those of the tree lights and one of the table lamps, it gave the room a wonderful atmosphere, and Izzy said she wished it could always be like this. Kate and James both added their grown up wisdom, saying that she would soon tire of it if it was always like this and it would not be special if it happened all time.

James added: didn't she always love the spring when the new lambs came and the summer when she could ride Muffin in the paddock? To which Izzy agreed, reluctantly.

"Yes, but isn't Christmas the most exciting thing, Dad?"
Izzy persisted. "Especially this one, not counting, of course, that Grandpa and Grandmas aren't here, and won't get to meet Kate."

"You know, Izzy, I hope I never forget this Christmas, and for all the right reasons: and you and your dad are all the right reasons," said Kate.

Izzy was puzzled at what Kate had said, but somehow she knew it was good.
"Okay Izzy, do you not think it's time for bed? Or you will not get to sleep before Santa Clause comes."

Izzy jumped up faster than she would any other night. She leaned over to Kate and kissed her on the cheek and said, "Merry Christmas Kate, I'm so glad you're here! And I hope Santa Claus brings you some presents…"

"Thank you, Izzy. I don't think Santa will know I'm here, but that's a really kind thought.

Merry Christmas to you, and sleep well, I'll see you in the morning."

James followed Izzy up the stairs, chatting away to her about going to sleep quickly so that morning would come before she knew it. Kate heard laughter as they got to Izzy's bedroom, and part of her wished she could be a fly on the wall, listening to what they were saying.

When James came back downstairs, he pointed out that Izzy was lit up like a firefly and unlikely to sleep for at least half an hour, to which they both laughed. Most children would stay awake for hours, but Izzy, even lit up, would be dead to the world in minutes, so half an hour was *extremely* excited for her. James had carried a bottle of wine and two glasses in for them. He poured a glass each and then flopped down into his favorite chair.

"You look exhausted, James. I feel so guilty – I have slept most of the day and feel as though I could still sleep on a clothes line."

James yawned and then apologized, "No, no. I'm fine. But I will not get any lie in tomorrow morning, as Izzy will be up at the crack of dawn. I would advise you to get as much sleep as you can, because tomorrow will be exhausting. Take my word for it. You go up; I have one or two things to do before I go. I need to settle the dogs, and one or two other things."

"Are you sure I can't help you?"

James refused, saying it was nothing and that he wouldn't be long.

"Oh, and in case I forget to tell you Kate, you look so much better tonight," James said, taking a long look at this woman who, three days ago, he would not have given a second thought toward.

Chapter 9

Kate woke to someone gently but firmly rocking her shoulder back and forth.

"Wake up, Kate. Wake up. It's Christmas morning. We have to see if Santa Claus has been here."

"Sorry, what? Erm, who?" said Kate, gradually coming out of the deep, comfortable sleep she was in, to see Izzy kneeling on her bed and saying something.

"It's Christmas morning, Kate. You must come down stairs – Grandma and Grandpa always come downstairs, and we all open our presents together. Come on!"

By this time, Kate realized what was happening, and rallied her senses enough to remember what Christmas was like for a child of seven. She turned toward Izzy, and with as much enthusiasm as she could muster said, "Okay, I'm awake. Go and wake your father up. Give me a minute to brush my teeth."

Izzy ran off and repeated the same procedure with her father. Minutes later they all met on the landing, looking bleary eyed and still half asleep, except Izzy, who was bursting with energy. As all three of them walked down the stairs, Kate and Izzy looked through the spindles of the banister, and Kate could not believe the transformation in the lounge since she had gone to bed. Izzy gasped: "Oh Dad! He's been!" cried Izzy.

Izzy ran down the remaining stairs into an array of festive decorations and Christmas lights. A garland from a spruce tree had been fixed across the large, heavy beam, above the fire place, and the scent of spruce filled the room. Attached to the branches were three long woollen socks filled with all kinds of lumpy things, if the shapes were anything to go by, and a large fat orange sticking out of the top of each one, adding to the wonderful collection of smells in the room.

The tree lights, and the glow from the fire, were the only lights in the room, giving it a magical atmosphere. Kate could never remember having a Christmas such as this when she was a child. It brought tears to her eyes knowing that James cared so much for his daughter – that even though he had been exhausted last night, he had stayed up to create this wonderland, especially for his little girl to wake up to. As Izzy had explained to Kate the day before, her array of presents were indeed laid out on the sofa in front of the fire. James opened the fire doors, and the heat spilled out, as they all took their places sitting on the hearth to keep warm.

"Are you okay sitting down there Kate?"

"Oh yes, I'm fine. Honestly James." Kate looked directly at James and smiled an affectionate smile full of admiration.

"Wow, this is lovely James! You are a wonderful father. I suppose everyone knows that?"|

"Ha! Don't go bandying it around – I am supposed to be a tough farmer."

By this time, Izzy had opened one of her presents and squealed with delight at what looked to Kate like a plastic box. Puzzled, but seeing how pleased Izzy was, she knew that there must be more to it than she could see.

"Oh Dad! Thank you, thank you! Thank you, it's perfect!"

Izzy looked at Kate and said, "It's an incubator Kate; now I can hatch my own eggs, and have chicks from my very own hens. Isn't it wonderful?"

"Wow!" Kate said, "That's great, Izzy…" rather amused by the gravity of the excitement shown by Izzy.

"Now you open a present, Dad. It's your turn."

"Okay. What have I got here?" James said in an exaggerated way, as he opened a present clearly wrapped by his daughter. "Oh, Izzy! Wow, that's lovely," he said in all seriousness, as he opened the present to reveal a slim box holding a lovely silver pen, with the name *James* engraved on it."

"It's for when you do your writing, Dad. Grandma got it engraved for me in Edinburgh."

James leaned over to his daughter and kissed her on the head, saying with all seriousness, "Thank you, Isabella. I will treasure it. I really will. Now it's Kate's turn".

Kate looked mystified – how on earth? Izzy went behind the tree to collect two presents which had been hidden at some point.

"Open one," said Izzy.

"Oh, how kind of you both! I didn't expect anything. I have nothing for either of you."

"Don't get your hopes up, it's nothing too exciting; but it's kindly meant from both of us," said James.

Kate opened the wrapper without actually picking up the parcel, as it was very heavy. As she tore the Christmas paper open from the top, she could see it was a ceramic, oblong, container filled with soil, and a little sign which had been hand made in the style of a 'for sale' sign, and read: *Think of us when these are in bloom*. Merry *Christmas from James and Izzy. XXXXX*.

"They are daffodils, Kate. They will look lovely in the spring. It's for your windowsill – It's a window box, isn't it, Dad?"
said Izzy, who was as excited by Kate's present as she was by her own.

"I don't know how to thank you, it's lovely. Thank you both very much, and I will certainly think of this day when they bloom on my windowsill in my little flat in Manchester." Kate swallowed hard.

"It's your turn again, Izzy," said Kate, giving herself time to get over the kindness of these two people who knew nothing about her, and to whom she had brought nothing but trouble to their door, yet they continued to surprise her with their generosity of spirit.

"Oh my, Oh my! Oh Dad, this is too much!"

Izzy unwrapped an enormous lamp with a long chain on it.

"Oh Dad, that's fantastic! I can't wait to get started; it's a heat lamp, Kate, for my baby chicks when they hatch."

"Oh … wow. I, erm, would never have guessed. You are good for my education, Izzy – these are all new to me, and I will learn from your expert tuition all about chickens."

They all laughed, and of course it was James' turn again, and he opened yet another Izzy wrapped present, which was a massive tin of liquorices of all sorts, as, apparently, as James admitted, he had a weakness for them.

Then Kate was given her other present, which was smaller but just as heavy. She had an idea that it was another ceramic pot – this time it had a little wigwam over the top of clear plastic, and it was indeed another beautiful ceramic plant pot, and again the sign read: *Think of us when you smell this scent. Merry Christmas from James and Izzy.*

"Its hyacinths Kate, and when you get back to your flat, you had better put them in a cupboard for a little while until shoots are showing, then take the plastic wigwam off. Then you can put it anywhere and the flowers will come out. They smell lovely in the spring, I hope you like them.

"Do you know these are my favorite presents? And I'm not just saying that, you couldn't have bought me anything that means more to me than these, and I will always think of you both in the spring when they flower. The ceramic pots are fabulous; don't tell me you make them as well? I would love to buy something like this for my flat."

"Oh, Morag makes the pots. She makes all kinds of stuff; she is good, isn't she? She has made me a man made out of plant pots for my little garden at the front of the house, though he is covered in snow at the moment," informed Izzy.

The present opening continued. Everything Izzy was given got the same amount of excitement: a rug for Muffin, a selection box of sweets, then her presents from her Grandma and Grandpa, which had been sent on earlier when they had realized that they would not make it for Christmas morning. When Izzy squashed the package she said in a knowing way, "It's clothes. I wonder what it is?" as she tore the paper off quickly. She was delighted with a pair of pink pajamas with little horses on them and a little box, which held the matching slippers. But when Izzy opened the next parcel from her grandparents, she held the item of clothing up in total awe, exclaiming how beautiful it was. It was a deep sapphire, blue velvet dress, with three quarter length sleeves and a heart shaped neck. In the same parcel was a pair of white tights to go with it.

"Oh Dad! Isn't it lovely? Oh I wish Grandpa and Grandma were here so I could tell them how much I love it. Oh, it's so grown up and posh, isn't it Dad? I can't wait to wear it – we will have to go somewhere really special for me to wear it, Dad. I will ring them straight away to wish them merry Christmas, and … Oh! I can't – the phone is down, isn't it?"

"And, young lady, I can almost bet that your Grandpa and Grandma are still in the land of nod – this is the first Christmas that you have not thrown them out of their bed at this ungodly hour, and if they have any sense they will still be asleep. You can ring them as soon as the phone lines are connected again."

There was a lot more present opening: sensible things for James such as socks, and the usual sweater from his mother and a pair of warm pajama – his mother had a thing about keeping warm, said James, as he unfolded the quite stylish nightwear, which looked more like a track suit.

"Mothers think you are going to freeze to death if you don't wear pajamas. Talking of pj's, whatever that is your wearing, it's the most colourful … giant ... baby grow? I've ever seen."

Kate looked down at her combination long johns which had stripes of every colour in the rainbow and said, pretending to be very serious, "And what's wrong with my pj's?"

And they all burst out laughing. Izzy rolled onto the floor laughing, saying, "I think they are great, and I would love some … whatever they are…? But they are the funniest things I've ever seen."

"Well," said Kate, "I bought them to go under my skiing clothes. They are called: all in one, combination, long johns. They are the warmest thing I had to sleep in."

"But where are your proper pajamas, Kate?"

Asked Izzy innocently, and Kate coughed slightly and said, "Well, I must have forgotten to pack them," glancing up at James, who realized that Kate would not think she was in need of nightwear when she was with her boyfriend on a romantic holiday.

"Anyway, who needs pj's when they have long johns?"

"Well they certainly are colourful. And who would have thought they could look as sexy as they do on you?" James said smiling, while running his eye over her figure hugging attire appreciatively.

While Izzy and Kate sat in front of the fire, chatting about each of the presents they had received, James went through to the kitchen and made coffee. He brought everything through on a tray, and Kate was struck once again at how domesticated he was. She almost said to herself 'for a man', but of course he was both mother and father to Izzy, and as such, knew all about what little girls needed far better than she herself would. They sat with their drinks, telling Kate what they had bought for Grandpa and Grandma and things that had happened on previous Christmas mornings. Eventually James said, "Well, Christmas or not, I still have animals to feed, so I think we should collect all this wrapping paper and get dressed. Breakfast is usually a lazy affair on Christmas day, and my mother and father usually do the honors but..."

"I can make breakfast James. I am not a bad cook, you know, for a city girl, and I'm feeling so much better this morning. I might even try leaving the strapping off my ribs today. What do you think?"

"Nope, I think that's pushing it. And you only feel better because you felt so rotten before. You can make the breakfast, but I don't want you to overdo things. It's less than a week since you were very … well, poorly, shall we say."

Kate agreed and knew that James was right, but she wanted to return the kindness that this family had shown her. James said he would be about an hour and a half, so that gave Kate plenty time to shower and change. In the meantime, Izzy had put everyone's Christmas presents under the tree, then she must have dressed at the speed of light, as she was outside with James by the time Kate came downstairs. Kate was dressed in a pair of denim jeans and a soft wool sweater of delicate pink with cropped sleeves and a short waist, which complimented her trim figure. After laying the table, Kate looked into the fridge to see what there was to cook with. Naturally there were loads of eggs and bacon, so Kate decided on a pile of toast and bacon and eggs. She knew the time had come for her to be brave and use the hot plates, this cooker was not going to get the better of Kate Johnson, she said out loud. In no time at all, Bacon was sizzling, and eggs ready to go in the pan. As soon as James and Izzy came in from the barn, toast was piled high, and the coffee was heating on the stove.

Whilst going through the fridge for breakfast food, Kate came across all the makings of Christmas dinner, which Lorna had kindly sent for them. As Lorna hadn't any idea that James and Izzy were not alone, she had made the meal as simple as possible, and it looked as though it simply needed heating up, all except the turkey, which was dressed and ready for the oven. Kate hunted round until she found a very large metal cooking tin, in which she placed the turkey. She layered the turkey with bacon and smeared it all over with butter, which was the way she would normally cook her own. She then covered it with tinfoil and placed it into one of the ovens, remembering James' advice: that once you opened the door the heat hit you in the face, so it was best to stand back for a second.

James and Izzy came in just as Kate was about to fry the eggs, and as they opened the kitchen door, they both took a deep breath and sniffed in the wonderful smell.

"There is something special," James said, "about coming in to a meal you haven't cooked for yourself. It must be a childhood thing from when your mother made you meals. However, my mother is a wonderful woman and a lovely cook, but when I was growing up, she and dad were really busy running their practice, and I had a lot of DIY meals. So it's a real treat to have you here, and cooking for us is a bonus, isn't it, Izzy?"

"Hey you haven't tasted my food yet. It might be horrible, and then what will you say?"

"Well," said Izzy, "I will say: at least it smelled lovely, and you tried your hardest. What more can you do?"

"Oh bless you, James. I'm going to take her home with me – she is perfect: she is beautiful, well mannered, and very generous."

"Oh, I couldn't let her go … unless of course I got a good price for her…"

Izzy squealed with laughter, "You horrid thing! You wouldn't sell me, would you?"

James put his long arms around Izzy and said, "Not even for a million pounds."

"Or a trillion," said Izzy, and so it went on as they all chatted light heartedly until breakfast was finished.

"Well, now we can both safely say you are a wonderful cook and that we would like to hire you as a housekeeper."

"Oh, that would be the best thing ever, wouldn't it, Dad?"

"Ha! Don't make snap decisions – I may take you up on that one day."

Kate said to James that she had put the turkey in the oven but she wasn't sure how the temperature worked on such devils fires as those ovens. The rest, she explained, would just heat up when the time came to eat, so if he just said roughly when he wanted to eat, giving the turkey about four hours should do it.

"Put your coat on madam, I think it's time you had some fresh air and rest, away from the cooker. You've done more than enough and I will take care of dinner. You're supposed to be resting. You look much better, but that is not to say that you are healed. Come on, I'll show you the calves, if you can stand the noise."

"Oh, and Kate, I will show you where I am going to put my incubators for the eggs, and hang my new heat lamp. Oh, I can't wait until I get some chicks – they will be my first, my very own! You will love them, Kate."

Kate had to stop herself from making the obvious reply, that she would be long gone by then. She knew at some point when the snow let up she would have to take her leave and go back to her life. The thought filled her with dread, and she realized that at this moment she simply could not face it. She didn't want the snow to melt. She was happier in these last few days than she ever thought she could be again.

Christmas dinner was cooked by James, who insisted that she stay in the living room with her feet up resting until she was called. After all, he said, not only was she not fit yet, but also she had been out of bed since the crack of dawn and needed the rest. When Izzy came through to tell Kate to come now because dinner was ready, she led Kate by the hand, and Kate had a feeling it was going to be something special, as the little girl was bristling with pride. As Kate and Izzy walked in the door and Kate had her first glimpse of the beautifully laid table, she noticed that the glow from two large red candles made it look far from the breakfast table of that morning. There were crackers, cloth napkins, wine glasses, and the smell, which had tantalized her even as she had dozed on the sofa. That same smell was now overpowering, and it was making her tummy rumble.

"Oh, it all looks gorgeous! Don't tell me you did all this on your own?"

"Oh no, I had my expert assistant, without whom I could not have managed," James said proudly, holding his hand out towards Izzy, indicating his assistant.

Izzy took a bow. As they laughed, Izzy showed Kate where she must sit just, as they do in restaurants, and Kate dutifully sat down, while James served the delicious smelling food to each of them.

Before they started their meal, James poured each of them a drink, and he held his glass up in the air, and for a split second, he looked from one to another then said: "A Merry

Christmas to all of us, and may the New Year bring good health and happiness to each and every one of us," which brought cheers and applause from Kate and Izzy.

Kate would not have believed it if someone could have predicted how happy she could be after such a horrendous, life changing event. The black cloud still hung over her like a prison sentence, and she knew it had to be faced, but for the present she managed to push it to the back of her mind.

After dinner, it was a typical Christmas of lazing in front of the fire. The thing that distinguished this house from city life was that, instead of having Christmas day television on, James, Izzy and Kate were playing the cheating kind of monopoly – the more they cheated the more they laughed, until Izzy eventually began to yawn.

James suggested that she put her new pyjamas on, then she would be ready for bed and she could read for a while. The day had flown over, and it was hard to believe that it was seven thirty in the evening and pitch dark outside. James got up and stood looking out at the moon, commenting that it was almost like daylight. Kate went over to look out of the window and stood close to James in a companionable way, saying in amazement how beautiful it looked. Kate said she knew that it was bringing everything to a standstill on the roads and in the cities, but it was spectacular, especially up here, where you are detached from the world. Her words held a wealth of meaning, which they both knew and understood

Izzy came down the stairs in her lovely new pink pyjamas with little horses on and matching slippers.

"I almost don't want to sleep in them, in case they get spoiled, Dad. But they are so lovely and warm and they smell lovely, so I'm going to be lovely and cozy in them. She picked up a magazine and kissed James goodnight, then she went over to Kate and kissed her cheek, and said with real sincerity, "I have had a lovely Christmas Kate, and I thought it was going to be so sad without Grandpa and Grandma. But you have made it really special."

"Thank you, Izzy. You and your Dad have made this the best Christmas ever for me, and I am not kidding. I mean that."

Kate took a hold of the magazine that Izzy had and glanced at the title; she had to laugh. "Most little girls would have a child's magazine, or a comic, or a Roald Dahl, but what does your daughter have?"

"Your *Practical Poultry Guide*. I love it. I simply love her to bits," Kate said, as Izzy ran up the stairs laughing at Kate's reaction to her magazine.

Chapter 10

As James and Kate sat in front of the log fire with a relaxing glass of wine, it took Kate a second to work out what had happened. Suddenly everything had gone dark: the tree lights had gone out and so had the table lamps in the corner of the room.

Izzy shouted down the stairs that she had just opened her book and, would you believe it, the power had gone off. James shouted okay, and then said to Kate, "Oh, don't worry. It's nothing to panic about. It happens all the time, especially when there's heavy snow on the cables. Just sit tight, I will get the tilly lamps lit and I will nip up and light one for Izzy, so she can read, although she will be asleep in two minutes, so it's hardly worth it."

James went and got one of, what Kate thought, was the most old-fashioned lamps she had ever seen. She thought he must have inherited them with the farm they looked so old-fashioned. James seemed to pump a plunger thingy a couple of times; he lifted the glass and lit the white thing, which looked like lace, which apparently is called a mantle, according to James. Suddenly the lamps popped and gave out the brightest yellow light, and a steady hissing noise, which although scary at first, James assured her, you would not notice after a minute. He took one lamp upstairs for Izzy and put the other lamp on the shelf above the fire place. It was amazing how much light came out of it. Kate asked if they were very old, as she had never seen anything like it. Actually, she would have been afraid to light it herself, what with the popping and hissing, but it seemed to give off a wonderful and efficient light, and quite a lot of heat.

James and Kate sat in front of the fire in a comfortable silence, before Kate said, "Don't you miss being a journalist James? I can see that you love farming, but what a massive life change it is. Did you give it up to look after Izzy?"

James seemed to pause a minute before answering, giving just enough time for Kate to say she was sorry and it was none of her business, and that she didn't mean to pry but it was just an observation, and really none of her business.

"No, I would like to tell you. It's time I said it out in the open. I think it may help me, as you telling me your story probably helped you a little." The last was said with a query in his voice, to which she nodded in agreement.

"Really, it started before I went to University: my parents thought that I would take law and follow them into the ready made business. However, it wasn't that I was being deliberately rebellious, as teenagers are, it was that I always had a yearning for far away places and was equally good at telling stories. So I took journalism at University. To cut a long story short, I became a freelance reporter, to begin with. I sold my stories to anyone who would pay me money. I barely scraped a living, but I was doing what I wanted to do, following the dream I told myself.

"Gradually, my name became known, and I was able to name a price, and afford to live on the money I earned. I soon realized that the kind of stories that sold were those of war, death, and the atrocities of war. And, for a while, I seemed to drift from one atrocity to another, until I decided to move on to Asia. There I uncovered sweat shop workers – young children being kept in work houses and paid a pittance for their labor. This lead me to India, and automatically to the poverty stricken areas of Mumbai. From there I covered earth quakes and floods; seeing bodies either crushed under buildings or washed up on river banks, until the stench of death seemed to fill my lungs and permeate my skin. One morning, I woke up in some stinking hotel room, which for some, in whatever country I was in, would have thought was luxury, but in actual fact it was squalor. I became sick to my stomach of it all: the death, the pointless waste of lives in never ending wars, where only the innocent suffer. The acts of God, which seemed to be all around, treating human life with no more importance than flotsam and jetsam. So there and then I decided to go back to England.

I took a job at a National Newspaper which I acquired without problem, as I had by then a fairly high profile reputation. I truly think, when I look back, that I was close to a break down. However, you don't recognize these things yourself, so I worked at the paper for a while and was relatively happy. That was when I met Jennifer. She was an aspiring reporter, and in hindsight, I should have known that her attraction to me was not love. It was admiration: hero worship for the journalist, not the man.

But I suppose I was flattered, in a way: she thought that I was this famous war correspondent, which was everything she wanted to be. We had a whirlwind courtship, and I was so desperate to have a normal life, I had seen so much misery and death, that I wanted to settle down. I realize now that it was a mistake and that I was not being fair to Jennifer, but I couldn't see that at the time.

"We got married, and every time I was offered a post away, I managed to field it off with some excuse or another. Jennifer got more and more frustrated with me for not taking assignments which she would have given her eye teeth for. Then, what seemed to me to be the perfect way out, came in the form of my parents. My mother wrote to me and told me that Dad and she were seriously thinking of selling

Comraich, as the farm manager, who had managed the farm since I was a boy, was retiring. They didn't think they would find anyone as hard working and loyal again. At their age they got over to the house less and less these days, and unless I wanted to inherit it, they asked it I would have any objections to them selling it.

"You see, Kate, you haven't had a chance to see it all yet, but Comraich is five thousand acres: the manor house, which Mother and Dad lived in, and which Jennifer and I lived in for a couple of years until she left; the farm, which Izzy and I now live in, as it's more convenient and more comfortable for two people; and the two tenant farms. Comraich was a lifetime's commitment for my parents; they took it on as part of a divorce settlement debt.
When they went up from Edinburgh to see what they had been lumbered with, it was almost a derelict property. However, they fell in love with it on sight and spent most of my life renovating it to its former glory.

"It was at that time that Jennifer was absolutely shell shocked to find out she was pregnant with our child. She was furious: she threatened to have an abortion. She said her career had not even started and she didn't want to be saddled with a child. We argued, and I tried my best to calm the situation, as I was thrilled with the thought of being a father – it was everything I had wanted: a wife, a baby, and now the perfect opportunity had arisen; one which had not really crossed my mind and yet had been staring me in the face. I wanted to go home. Suddenly, I had this yearning to go home, now, immediately. I persuaded Jennifer that, if she came with me, I could look after the baby while she did free lance work. That it was no different than before, because I would stay with the baby instead of her.

"She agreed, reluctantly, having no other way out. We packed everything up in Manchester, with obscene haste on my part, and left for Comraich. Well, to cut a long story short, Jennifer never liked it. She hated the farm element of it, she detested the isolation, and to make it worse, once she had left the paper she had become invisible as far as work went. She had not been in the business long enough to have established her name as a freelance correspondent. Oh, she did the odd article from home and managed to sell enough to keep her hand in, not for the money, we didn't need that, but for the reputation angle.

"Isabella was born. But instead of making things better, it seemed to drive an even bigger wedge between us. Jennifer resented Izzy for spoiling her chances of having a career, and it was as though Izzy sensed Jenny's coolness towards her, and she and I just seemed to gravitate to each other. Izzy was like my shadow: where I went, she wanted to go. She was a wonderful baby: she was happy, she loved the outdoors; in fact, you couldn't keep her in, which didn't please Jennifer, as she hated the countryside.

"I on the other hand had never been so happy. I spent my days working on the land, using my hands, and generally being useful and productive."

James sighed, then carried on talking.

"However, Jennifer was more and more unsettled, and we began to argue more and more, as it was becoming very clear she wanted to go back to her life in Manchester. The thoughts of leaving this life, and taking Isabella to live in a pokey little flat in Manchester, was so abhorrent to me – and Jenny knew this – that there seemed to be no way of compromise.

"Then, one day after being out in the fields with Izzy, we came back and Jennifer had gone! She had just packed her bags and gone. She left a note to say that she handed over all parental guardianship of Izzy to me, as in her heart she knew that it was Izzy I loved and not her, and that, in all honesty, she felt the same way. She said that she could never be happy and she had known it from the day she got pregnant. She had no need to tell me how disappointed she was in me, as I was not the man she thought I was when we married.

"The thing is Kate, I could deny my part in our disastrous marriage, I could play the injured party – left with the baby to bring up on my own – but that would be totally untrue. After the initial shock of Jennifer leaving, there was a time when I actually felt relieved – yes, relieved – because there were no more arguments, no more strained atmosphere, and no more feelings of guilt. The feelings of guilt were mine, because

I know now looking back that I was ready for marriage, ripe for it in fact – after the horrors of Asia and India, I wanted the middle class marriage, family, home, and everything that went with safety and happiness. I look back and realize that I was broken in spirit and should never have married Jennifer; it was unfair of me to deny her the opportunity to do what I had done. I told myself that I was protecting her from the horrors that I had encountered, but I had no right to do that. She had her own life to live and her own mistakes to make, and I denied her those."

Kate wanted to intervene and tell him not to blame himself for everything, and that Jennifer had made her choice and must have loved him or she would not have married him. But she stayed silent, as he had done when was not ready to conclude her story, for neither was he.

"I have heard very little since the day Jennifer left. She does not send Izzy a birthday card or Christmas card. And at first, I thought she was being cruel, but I have now decided that she is not a cruel person, she simply decided that if she was not going to be part of Izzy's life then it would be cruel to send cards, giving Izzy the lingering hope that one day she would return.

"I did once read an article on the internet, where foreign correspondents write, which gives news services a chance to see who is out there and how good they are. The article had Jennifer's name on it, her maiden name to be precise. It was an excellent piece, and that was the last I heard of her. I don't blame Jennifer in any way, and I truly wish her happiness, as much happiness as Isabella and I have."

"I think you are being very hard on yourself James. I also think you are a kind and thoughtful man. I can see from Jennifer's point of view, I think, and in my humble opinion she had a choice and she made it. However, as we all know, in life we do not always make the right choices, and in Jennifer's case she appeared, if you don't mind me saying this, to be in love with the image of you rather than you as a person.

"You can tell me to mind my own business if you don't want me to comment, but I think when you were in Asia and India you saw 'too much': women can cry and release their pain, but men traditionally have had to keep everything bottled up. If the letter had come from your mum before you married Jennifer, the opportunity to come back to Comraich would have been there and you would have had time to heal. But life is not always as simple as that."

"Do you know what the meaning of Comraich is in English Kate, or Comric, as the English pronounce it?"

"No, I'm afraid I don't."

"Well, I'm going to tell you a little story, if you're not bored to death already…"

"No, no, James. I am not bored at all. I am here to listen, and if that's all I can do, after the kindness you have shown me, it's little enough."

"Well, you asked for it," he said with a wry smile. "The manor house, which you have not seen yet, was, as I say, in lieu of a debt, which was paid to my parents for the couple in question's divorce. Well, when my parents read all the paperwork that came with the house, it apparently had a very, very, unhappy past. At least three of the couples had divorced and sold

149

the property on. So, when my parents took it over and started to renovate it, they would travel up every weekend, and it became a labour of love to restore the house. However, my mother once told me, when Jennifer and I were going through a bad patch and it had become obvious to my parents, that dad and her went through a sticky patch where they just seemed to work and work and had no time together, prior to taking on Comraich. Then, something happened during the process of rebuilding the house and spending more time together. They started to enjoy each other's company again, as they had when they were younger: they took time out to have fun, something else which they had forgotten how to do while they were building their careers and the business. My mother told me that the thoughts I had been having about the house being unlucky were not true, because her and my father had proved there was no such thing as a curse. And after all, the name of the house is *Sanctuary* in English. This was my mother's way of trying to help me, trying to give me hope that every marriage has problems which have to be overcome. But, I'm afraid in my case it was never meant to be. However, Comraich was my sanctuary: it saved me from the horrors of war and gave me back my love of life," James said in a quiet, thoughtful voice.

Kate added, "And it saved my life for me – had it not been for Comraich and Elsa, I would have died."

They both sat silent for a moment, when all that could be heard was the hiss of the Tilly lamp and the crackle of the logs in the fire. James tenderly said, "You are the only person I have ever told the full story to. Oh, I told my parents about the marriage break up, the obvious things – that Jennifer wasn't happy here and needed to go back to her life, but I have never been able to go back to the time when I was in Asia and India; in fact, the pain was so deep of the death and the squalor which I saw, it wiped out any of the more pleasing parts of the continents. I know there must have been days when it wasn't all horror, but so far I have only had glimpses of those days in my memories, which I tend to shy away from as I am not ready to face them yet."

"You know what they say – you can talk to a stranger where you cannot tell a friend, so I suppose we have proved that. And I think we have been able to comfort each other; that helps me feel less guilty about falling out of the blue and landing on your farm at Christmas time."

"Ha! No, no, Santa Claus sent you to me for Christmas; Izzy said so."

"Then it must be true, because cherubs don't lie," said Kate.

They sat drinking wine and chatting easily, until the early hours. Until Kate told James they had better go and have at least a couple of hours sleep. He had to get up shortly for his round of feeding the animals, and she said in a gloating tone not to disturb her in her lovely warm bed. And with that they made their way to bed, James feeling as though a weight had been lifted from within. He had never shared the full story with anyone. To be honest, he thought he had never actually put it into words, or even allowed himself to think so fully about his time abroad, and it was with a feeling of relief that he went to bed that night.

Chapter 11

The day that followed James' and Kate's late night should have been one of exhausted slog for James: feeding animals after only a few hours sleep, but it wasn't. He felt happier than he had felt for ages: he whistled as he worked, as they say. For Kate, her feelings of desolation were not the same as they had been. Instead, she had the feeling that things were never as bad as they looked at the time they happened, and that the mess she was in was going to sort itself out, one way or another. But whatever the outcome, life was not all over for her, it was only just beginning.

Kate cooked breakfast while Izzy, who had been up bright and early and had, already, fed Muffin and her chickens, ran to tell her father breakfast was ready. James and Izzy came in together and commented on the lovely smell.

"I'm being spoiled," James said. "It has been a long time since anyone other than my mother has cooked for me, and you can not explain how nice it is to come into a room and have a meal put in front of you. That's the only bit about working on the farm that is hard: coming in after a hard day and no meal on the table; does that make me sound feudal?"

"No, I can understand that. It's not unlike when I get home to my flat and I have a freezer full of food but no inclination to cook for one. More often than not I will call at a restaurant and have a bite on the way home."

"Oh, that sounds so lonely," Izzy said.

"I hate to think of you on your own, Kate. I wish you lived near us and you could come here all the time."

"Thank you, Izzy. Do you know you say the kindest things?"

They ate breakfast and chatted about the day ahead. Izzy was going to fit her incubator and heat lamp up, and James said he would give her a hand when he had mucked out the cows. Kate, without thinking, said she would help Izzy if there were anything she could do.

An outsider could have easily mistaken this to be an ordinary family having a normal breakfast and planning their day. When breakfast was over, James and Izzy both said, "Thank you Kate, that was lush, in fact."

Izzy added, "I think it was as good as Dad's."

"Wow, praise indeed!" said Kate.

"Well, I have to agree with my daughter, especially because I did not even have to lift a finger. I will go one further and say I enjoyed it more than my own."

"Wow, Kate – you can definitely do the cooking from now on."

"Erm, I think somehow I have been duped…"

They all laughed as they left the kitchen. Kate loaded the dishwasher with a feeling of well being she had not felt in a long, long time.

Kate decided to put on Grandma's wellies and outdoor coat and walk to the barn. It was the first time she had walked very far, other than in the house, and although her ribs felt so much better now, they were still strapped for support. In the boot room she found a walking stick with a long handle, which apparently, she found out later, was a crook for working with the sheep. This, she thought, would steady her as she plodded through the still deep snow to the barn. She bypassed the ones with the noisy cows and calves in until she got to the one that housed the horses and Izzy's chickens.

Kate felt like a puny townie when she had to put her whole body weight behind her just to open the sliding barn door. Then the the same feeling arose again when she had to close it to keep out the wind and the light, drifting snow, which seemed to fall constantly now.

"Hello Sapphire," said Kate, as she walked slowly up to the horses' stall. Sapphire seemed to nod and blow air through her nostrils as a greeting, though of course that was not the case, it was simply that Sapphire acknowledged that Kate was there. Kate stroked her long nose and cheek, telling the horse how beautiful she was, and Sapphire's head nodded up and down, enjoying the attention from Kate. Kate walked down to where she could hear Izzy talking away to herself, as she planned where exactly she was going to put the incubators and heat lamp for her new venture of producing her own baby chicks.

"Hi, do you need any help? "

Izzy was in the next empty stall to her chickens and was unpacking her incubator and all the bits that appeared to go with it.

"Oh yes, please. Dad has brought me this old work bench to put the incubator on, and of course it has to be next to the electric socket so that it can be plugged in, and also for the lamp to be connected to. The unpacking is not the hard bit, it's reading the instructions. Dad said he would help as soon as he is finished, only I thought I could get things started before he comes."

Kate took it all very seriously, as Izzy was obviously in deadly earnest that she could do it all herself if only she could understand the instructions, which, to be fair, were meant for grown ups, not ambitious seven year olds with nothing more than enthusiasm. Kate and Izzy fitted all the bits together, and as Kate read out the instructions, Izzy became very animated and organized, which was more than Kate was. However, between the two of them, they managed to fit it all together, ready for use. Kate asked Izzy when the little chicks were hatched where they would go until they were big enough to join the other hens.

"Oh, Dad has a big crate he is going to bring in. We will put it on the bench and hang the light above it, and they will sit under the heat to keep warm for a few weeks. According to the poultry book, until they are big enough to go without heat then they can go outside. Dad is going to fit a hook on the beam just above the crate and then we are ready. Oh, I can't wait! Isn't it exciting, Kate?"

Kate was totally caught up in Izzy's enthusiasm. She had never actually done anything practical in her life; the only practical thing she had ever put her hand to was changing the bag on the vacuum cleaner. She began to see the enjoyment a person got from actually starting and completing something that had a purpose.

Izzy was showing Kate how tame her hens were when James came into the barn. The wind howled as he pushed open the barn door far enough to bring in the quad with the trailer hitched to it, bringing in the crate he had promised Izzy.

"Hi," he said to both of them, as he heaved the big crate into the stall where Kate and Izzy had been working. "Somebody has been busy. It looks as though you don't need me – it's all done."

"No, no. It's not. We just unpacked everything. Kate read the instructions and I put it together, but it would be best if you checked it, Dad. I might not have done everything right, and I don't want it to get damaged. That crate is great – we should get lots of chicks in there, and it's big enough for them until they are quite big, isn't it, Dad?"

"Yes, I think so."

Glancing at the incubator, he said he thought they had done a wonderful job, and he would hook the light up if Izzy got him his hammer and a hook. Izzy ran off to the tool box and James and Kate smiled at her total enthusiasm regarding, what most kids of today would call, work.

While James and Izzy were busy with the intricacies of the heat lamp, they didn't even notice Kate's absence. When she returned she had a flask, which she had found in the kitchen cupboard and had filled with hot chocolate. She also had three mugs and some toasted tea cakes, which she had covered in tin foil to keep warm. They all sat on the bails of hay and enjoyed the unexpected snack.

"You are spoiling us. What will we do when you are not here?" James said.

There was a pause before Izzy, with the innocence of a child, said, "Could you not stay here and live with us Kate? We would look after you, and not expect you to do much work. Dad and I would help, wouldn't we Dad?"

James smiled a knowing smile while taking in Kate's reaction.

Kate had almost forgotten how young Izzy was. She was so competent at farm tasks that Kate had clean forgot that she was a child, and small child at that, who came out with uncomplicated solutions to problems. Kate's eyes misted over for a second and she said to Izzy that she would absolutely love to, but she had a job and a flat and … Kate almost said a Fiancé, but, in all honesty, she did not think that part could ever be true again, of Dominic.

"Anyway," said Kate, "how is it going? When can you start incubating eggs, then?"

"Well, we could start now, but as Dad says, it's still very, very cold. Even with the incubator on. It would be best to wait until the snow went away. You know Kate, I love the snow, but I wish it would hurry up and go, because I'm dying to start with the eggs and get my very own chicks."

Kate on the other hand was in no hurry for the snow to go, because once the weather became clear enough for her to leave, she would have no excuse to stay.

The day passed very quickly and in the evening they had one of Lorna's wonderful meals from the freezer, to which Kate said she wished that Lorna could cook for her, as it was the best food she had ever tasted. Izzy dressed for bed, and as usual, within minutes of going to bed, was fast asleep. Kate had never known anyone go to sleep as fast as Izzy could.

Chapter 12

James and Kate sat in front of the fire with a glass of wine in hand.

"You are teaching me bad habits. Normally being on my own, I don't bother too much having a drink in the evenings. I had forgotten how nice and relaxing it could be to have a drink with a friend and talk about the day."

"Well, to be honest, sometimes when I get home I'm so tired that I fall asleep in front of the television, and if I have opened a bottle of wine, the glass is still full when I wake up to go to bed. Drinking on your own is not as enjoyable as sharing a drink with a friend. It's not the drink after all, is it? It's the company."

James didn't really want to touch on Kate's private life, which would entail bringing Dominic into the conversation, though he was curious about her parents. Kate had never mentioned them at all and had not talked about them being worried about her in her absence.

"And your parents, Kate? Are they alive?"

"My father is. He lives in Greece with his currant partner, and he has a villa over there. He has lived abroad in one way or another since I was a child. My father and mother divorced when I was young. My mother was Spanish and she went back to Spain to live with her family when I was very young, so I don't know if she is still alive. My father was a tour guide, a sort of courier, they used to call them. He spent most of my childhood going away I remember, until, I suppose, my mother had had enough and she left him.

"So what happened to you then? Where did you live? Did you go with your father?"

"Go with him? Ha! You must be joking. That would have cramped his style, having a child with him. Oh no, my father left me with my long suffering grandparents, to bring up." Kate said, not in an angry way but in a way that showed she was under no illusion about her fathers' selfish philandering ways, and that she had come to terms with it long ago.

"Oh, don't get me wrong, I don't blame my grandparents. They weren't cruel or anything. They did the best they could, but they were old and they had brought up their own child and didn't want to start again at their age. After going to college I took extra evening classes in business and finance and I found I had a real aptitude for it. I got a job in Manchester and after a while I moved into digs. Then onwards and upwards, so to speak: I now have a really high powered job and a lovely apartment in the Centre of Manchester. Over the last two years both my grandparents have died. My father didn't even fly over for their funerals, he sent a telegram, would you believe it? In this day and age. Saying he was sorry but he could not get away due to business commitments…"

James didn't know how to express the sadness he felt for Kate, having such a soulless upbringing, when he himself had such a happy childhood. His mother and father were the perfect parents. In fact they probably over compensated for the fact that they were so busy during the week building their practice: on weekends they tried their hardest to make the renovation of the house and the farm as much fun for James as for themselves. They bought James, Merlin, his very first horse, and what little boy wouldn't be happy playing on a farm and having a real live horse to play cowboys and Indians. He was always encouraged to take a friend with him so that he had lots of company. James' memories of his childhood were very happy and he suddenly had the overwhelming urge to comfort Kate. He leaned forward on the edge of his seat and took both of Kate's hands into his and looked down into her upturned face. Next, before he knew what he had done, his lips had gently touched Kate's soft mouth. Kate's lips barely had time to respond before the contact ended. The sudden realization of what had just happened made James cough slightly, standing at the same time, saying he had better go to the barn and have a last look at a young heifer which was about to calve. He told Kate not to wait up for him, as he may be all night.

"There is no telling how long she will take as it's her first. So I'll see you in the morning, err, okay?"

James felt slightly uncomfortable, however, no more so than Kate, who wondered what had just happened.

"Oh, yes, ok. I'll see you in the morning then, I hope everything goes all right for her."

And with that they both parted. Kate was left to wonder why he had kissed her and to analyze whether she liked it or not. Who was she kidding – she liked it, but she was confused. She shouldn't have liked it. Wasn't she still in limbo about her relationship with Dominic. The sudden realization came clearly to Kate; actually, no, she thought, there is no confusion about Dominic and herself, it was over. How could she possibly have any feelings for a man who could hit a woman, especially a woman carrying a child. She knew that the type of man who would hit a woman had always disgusted her and the fact that it was Dominic made no difference, and James was right that that type of violence would always surface in the end.

James stood inside the barn wondering what on earth he had done, kissing Kate like that. It was pointless – in a week or so she would be gone, back to her life in Manchester. He had only done it, he told himself, to comfort her for having such a lonely horrible life, not only when she was child, but even now with that pig of a fiancé, who had obviously beaten her up and left her for dead simply because she was expecting his child. Nevertheless, he could not help but think to himself that he had enjoyed the kiss, no matter how brief it had been. And Kate did not pull away either so she had obviously not found it distasteful. Oh, what was he doing? Was he so desperate for a woman he was clinging to straws now? James tried to put it to the back of his mind and get on with helping the poor heifer to calve.

Kate did go up to bed, but she knew sleep would be impossible. She needed something to take her mind off the turmoil it was in. She remembered seeing a bookcase full of books in the little cupboard on the landing which had been made into an office nook. It was the spot where James kept all of his computer equipment, and lots of files, which she assumed were farm paperwork. On one whole wall a shelving unit had been fitted and it was crammed full of books. Kate loved books and she was sure that if anything could take her mind off that kiss, browsing through someone else's choice of books would help. She did think that a persons' choice of book reflected what type of person they were.

Kate browsed for awhile until she came across a book by an author she had never heard of, which wasn't that unusual as the name was foreign: *The Underbelly of Asia* by Jody Wang. Kate flicked through the book and decided she would take it to bed and try to blot out her crowded thoughts by reading. As Kate started to read it became clear that the title of the book led you into a world of poverty, the prostitution of children, commercial sex, and the criminal networks that weaved its way through the socially rundown areas of Asia. Before Kate realized, she was deep into the author's portrayal of the life of a child from a poor district and the pimps that controlled their lives. Once in a while a human interest chapter would give a fleeting glimpse of the child before he or her was sold into the never ending poverty, which was to be their destiny.

So absorbed was Kate in what she was reading that from time to time she was unaware of her tears, which ran silently down her face for the innocence of the children and the inescapability of pain, which was inevitable. Kate read on and on until the early hours of the morning until drained and mentally exhausted. She came to the last page of the book. She took a deep sigh at the end of the book, and thought back to what James had said to her about being sick to his stomach, of it all, and the need to be cleansed of it by coming home. Suddenly, it came to her in a flash. She got up, and even though it must have been at least three-thirty in the morning, she crossed the landing and went back to the little computer room where the light was still lit. This indicated to Kate, that James must still be in the barn with the calving cow.

Kate looked through the shelves of books, quickly scanning for the author who she held in her hand, and sure enough, there was another one. This time it was called *Incredible India*, by Jody Wang. Kate took the book to bed with her, and though she was shattered, she began to see if the style of writing was the same.

She had a quick glance through the first chapter and it confirmed her suspicions: Jody Wang … Jody Wang … JW … James Wallace!

Kate was sure that these books had been written by James as a form of catharsis: a self healing and a way of dealing with what he had seen. The glimpses in the first book of the human side of the country and the sweetness of the children, before life forced them into its grip of necessity, was, she was sure, his way of trying to remember the kinder side of Asia.

She felt sure that when she was finished the second book she would find the same thread of a search for humanity among the abject poverty within the countries depicted. Kate eventually fell asleep, which at the beginning of the evening she thought she would never be able to do, given her last encounter with James.

Chapter 13

Breakfast time seemed to be hectic and both James and Kate were probably grateful for the distraction. The heifer had calved, but not until five in the morning, and she had not had a particularly easy birth. James was tired but uncomplaining. Izzy chatted away as normal during breakfast and couldn't wait until she could get started with the chicks. "Did you know," Izzy said, "I could hatch eighteen eggs in my incubator? Just think of that!" she chattered on, saying she would have eighteen little chicks of her very own, bred by her.

James and Kate loved Izzy's chattering this morning as it gave them both time to face each other without the need for a post mortem over the kiss of the night before. It would of course have to be mentioned, but neither of them was quite ready yet. Kate, in actual fact, had more on her mind, and was not sure how she was going to tackle her discovery. When breakfast was over, James said he would be in the barn this morning if Kate needed him for anything. Izzy would also be in the barn with her chickens and Muffin.

Kate said she would bring over a flask for elevenses if they fancied, and both James and Izzy laughed, saying, you have got to be joking, we would die for ready made elevenses, and they went off happily into the ever-deepening snow. When Kate looked at the deep snow, somewhere deep inside she knew that she was happy that it had not started to thaw. She was being given this opportunity to see a side of life that she would never have come across in her city life. She realized that if it were not for the circumstances in which she found herself here she wouldn't have met these wonderful people, she would love every minute. She really cared for Izzy … and James. The hesitation, when thinking of James, was because she was aware that she was developing feelings for him and was unaware as to what type of feelings.

Were they protective feelings because of what he had been through? Or was it simply hero worship as Jennifer had felt? Or was it something deeper? She thought for a moment: he was a kind, generous, gentle, and intelligent man. And who was she trying to kid, he was beautiful to look at. Suddenly, it dawned on her that he had made her heart race almost from the time her ribs stopped hurting, yet James still strapped them for support. Kate knew she needed to know more about James, and she felt that the window into him as a person lay in his written work. By now she was convinced that James Wallace was Jody Wang.

Before she had to take out the flask for elevenses, she had time to read a chapter or two of *Incredible India*. The time flew by as she read about the lives of those people: men, women, and children, who made their living in the slums of Mumbai. Glancing at her watch she realized she had been reading for two hours and was as fascinated by this book as she had been the last. The writer touched on the lives of ordinary people and told the story almost through their eyes, helping your imagination take the reader through the filthy streets with no sanitation, and yet, where whole families lived and worked. Kate had to drag herself away from the fascinating insight into the lives of the poorest of people, and bring herself back to reality. It was later than she had promised, but when she arrived, after plodding through the snow, carrying a basket full of goodies, both Izzy and James cheered.

"Oh, we thought you had forgotten about us!" said Izzy.

"Now would I do that? No, no, I've been reading and got totally lost in the fascinating lives of people in the far off lands of Asia and India," Said Kate, looking directly at James to see his reaction, and she was not mistaken in the look he returned. He did not look angry or upset, just amused by this woman that he had found lying in the snow in the middle of the night. There was more to her than met the eye, a great deal more, and he liked everything he saw so far, and would enjoy exploring further.

"Wow," said Izzy, breaking their eye contact, "bacon sandwiches! You are spoiling us. And they've got ketchup on. Dad, you can not let Kate go home, this is the best we have ever been looked after. Even when Grandma is here we don't get this treatment. Grandma says Dad has to watch his weight."

"You are so right Izzy, we will have to do all that we can to try and keep Kate here as long as we can."

Kate wandered up to Sapphire's stall and had a little talk to her. Well, not actually talk, but she did tell her again how lovely she was, and Izzy shouted up through the barn, "As soon as your ribs feel better, Kate, you should have a ride on Sapphire."

"No, no, I have never ridden a horse in my life, not even a donkey. Besides, the snow is too deep."

"If your ribs are better by later on in the week, you could at least ride up and down the barn and get used to how it feels to sit on a horse. Couldn't she, Dad?"

"Well, I don't see why not; we have a mounting block, which would help you get on without a problem, but you don't have to do it, Kate. Just because us country folk like horses doesn't mean that you have to. Thinking back to Jennifer and her pathological hatred of all things which had a tail, or fur, or, well, anything really – she just hated the country." He did not want to push Kate into doing something simply to please Izzy.

"Actually, maybe tomorrow or the next day, if my ribs don't hurt, I could just try sitting on Sapphire. Just sitting on her shouldn't be difficult, should it?"

"Yeah!" Izzy cheered. "You will love it. Once you have sat on a horse you will love it forever," said Izzy with childish enthusiasm.

When Kate went back into the house she went back upstairs to retrieve the book she had left on the dressing table. As she sat on the chair, in the bedroom opposite the mirror, Kate caught sight of herself. Her Eyes were bright, and the bruises around her eye were fading fast, and she had an animated look which she had not seen in herself for a long time. Oh yes, she had looked happy and excited when she found out she was pregnant, but it was because she was going to have something to love of her very own. That was a different kind of look: it's the look a woman gets when feeling maternal. This was different. It was a kind of sparkle, which emanated from within: she was happy and it showed, she thought. Then she told herself not to make such a big deal out of one kiss and a whole load of kindness from a handsome man.

By the time James and Izzy came in that evening, Kate had finished the book. She knew that she must speak to James about it – not only that she had taken the books from the bookshelf, but she hoped he was not upset with her for reading them without his permission. She thought this might bother James, as the books showed a side to him that only he could ever come to terms with: the side that was able to report the things he saw, and not be able to intervene and change the outcome. In a way, it's a bit like being a wildlife photographer, and filming while an animal is caught and killed when you could have prevented the kill. However, you would not be there the next time to change what is, after all, destiny.

After Izzy went to bed and James came into the living room with the wine and the coffee, he poured them a drink and sat down in his usual chair. After a moment of silence Kate started to apologize to James for reading the books without permission.

James stopped her in mid sentence: "No, if I didn't want them read then I would never have written them. I am, however, surprised that you managed to guess my secret about the pseudonym. I thought using a woman's name was a stroke of genius."

"Oh, it was, and I don't think anyone would ever have guessed, unless they knew of the history behind your life in Asia and India, and how it almost broke your spirit. I am taking a gamble here – and you must tell me to stop if I go too far – you had no need to put your name to the books because it was not for reviews or money that you wrote them, but as a way of bringing peace within yourself; peace after seeing those things that you saw and were not being able to do anything about except report them, for the world to read. It was the feeling of guilt over not having to live your life as those desperately poor people did; that all the time you knew that you could go home to where everything was clean and safe. That's the thing that hurt the most: the fact that they had no way out and you did."

James had tears in his eyes as Kate finished speaking. He swallowed hard and said to Kate, "When did you get to be so smart?"

They sat for a while and drank their wine while they both gathered their thoughts. "Do you know," James said, "I didn't think there were many people who could have pegged my reasons as correctly as you have," James said. "It was only after I had written those books after I came home that I felt able to move on and try to put the past behind me."

He had tried to explain to Jennifer, at the time, how the years had affected him and that he had no wish to go back or take any more assignments abroad. She never understood – all she could see was that he could work for any newspaper and they would pay him good money for those kinds of stories, which was all she ever wanted to do. James said that he hoped by now she understood how he felt and doesn't blame him for deliberately turning down and avoiding stories that she desperately wanted him to take.

I knew that avoiding those jobs probably contributed to the eventual break up of our marriage, as the gloss began to fall away from him as *the great correspondent*. And then all that remained was the man; a man who wanted to live on a farm, seemingly to retreat from life. James said he saw now that it was not fair for Jennifer, and he hoped she was as happy as he is now.

"After writing the books, it did give me a sense of peace. I tried to show the more human side to life. Oh, I don't mean that the sweat shops and the prostitution didn't come into it, they had to. It was part of the catharsis. But I hoped I was able to show a side to some of the children and young girls who I felt epitomized Asia, or rather the Asia of the bygone days, and the culture. If you left the cities' filth behind, there remained some extraordinarily beautiful scenery."

"I could see that. I sensed that in your books. I could picture the highs of the mountains and the lows of the paddy fields. And I cried over your depiction of the peasant farmers scratching a living, which in the end led to their young girls being sold into prostitution or a living as sweat shop workers."

"Shall I tell you what was extraordinary, Kate? The people I met in Mumbai, families, whole generations, lived on the rubbish tips. They were not miserable, and they didn't blame anyone for their plight. In fact, some of them knew nothing else and didn't know that their life was horrendous to a European. And if your stomach had the ability to not throw it up, they would share their last meal with you, right there on the tip. That's how wonderful and giving they could be.

"And children are children the world over, you would think, but in Asia their childhood is almost nil. By the time they have reached the age of seven, they practically knew what their future held. They may not have wanted to be part of the prostitution or the sex trade, but they knew no other way to earn money, and many of those children were keeping whole families alive, sending money back to the farms of their parents."

After a silence, which required no words, Kate eventually said to James, "Could you ever see the day when you could return to Asia or India as a tourist and not be able to think about what was behind the scenes?"

181

"No, no, I don't think I ever could. Don't get me wrong, the people were kind, hard-working, and on the whole happy, but it would not be the people that would stop me from going. It is the fact that, no matter how seemingly advanced the countries had become, I would always be aware at what price prosperity had been gained. And hidden behind the scenes it is always the poorest of society who are paying the price."

Without thinking, Kate stretched out her hand and laid it on James' arm, looking directly at him with her dark eyes, which were deep pools of emotion at that moment. She spoke to James, whose head was bent towards the floor, and said, "James, you are a kind and principled man, you have paid your debt to the people of Asia and Mumbai, for what, I'm sure, was a feeling of guilt that you were being paid to report on those situations you found so abhorrent. But you didn't create them, you only reported on them. And I know without reading any of them that it would have been done sympathetically and from the heart."

James's head rose and he looked directly into Kate's warm, dark eyes. At the same time he placed his hand over hers, saying, in order to lighten the mood a little, "I should be paying you, Kate Johnson from Manchester, too counsel me. I feel as though, for the first time, someone understands what I felt. And you have hit the nail on the head, and you have no idea how good it feels to hear someone say it out loud. Thank you, Kate. Now before we get all sentimental, I think it's time we went to bed, or it will be dawn again, or something else might happen, which needs a lot of thinking about."

And with that they both went off to bed, leaving Kate to think over what James had meant, about the something else, though she would be a fool if she didn't actually know what he meant. James went too bed too. He slept the sleep of the contented for the first time in a long, long time.

Chapter 14

New Year's Eve dawned bright and early with a clear blue sky. For the first time in over a week the sun shone and it was a glorious day. Izzy was in her bedroom, Kate was in the kitchen, and James was just coming in from the barn, telling Kate what a wonderful day it was, when they heard Izzy shouting down the stairs that she could see Eaden. She thought it was him on his tractor.

"Well, I think it's his tractor clearing the snow. He has the snow plough on and it's spraying snow high up in the sky," Izzy said, running down the stairs for breakfast.

At that moment the short wave radio, which was permanently switched on and kept on the desk in the corner of the kitchen, could be heard: "Hello, the house … hello. Get ready to receive orders for the New Years Eve party, which you are hosting tonight…" Morag's voice could be heard booming into the kitchen. "Don't worry," she told James and Izzy, "Lorna and I have the food all in hand. All you need to do is put your glad rags on and supply the booze."

James intervened into Morag's barrage of instructions to say, smoothly, "We have a visitor, so I hope you bring plenty of food, though she is not a bad cook herself…" James left the sentence hanging in the air and signed off, knowing that within seconds Lorna and Morag would be talking to each other, and trying to second guess who the female guest was, that was staying with him.

Kate was a little bit apprehensive about meeting James' neighbors and friends: the paragon Lorna, who cooked like a dream, and Morag, the arts and crafts person who makes beautiful pots, not to mention their husbands. She would feel a little like an intruder. Don't be silly, she thought to herself, she met people all the time in the course of her job and never gave it a thought. She had always been good with people, she was just being silly. She supposed she was still feeling a little fragile in the ego department.

"Oh dad, can I stay up for the party? Can I wear my new dress – the one Grandma gave me for Christmas? Oh, Kate! You will love Lorna and Morag, they are great fun. Aren't they dad?"

"Erm, well, actually, yes, they are great fun. And they are the best neighbors a single man could have. They have been very, very good to me and helped me out of a lot of awkward situations. Although they are my tenants, they are also my good friends."

Kate thought, well, I better get on with them, no pressure there then.

Breakfast was an excited meal, Izzy saying she couldn't wait to wear her new dress and tights, James saying he better get a move on and get things done, because knowing Eaden and Keith, they will be here early evening.

"Hey", said James, looking at Kate's worried face, "they are really, really nice people. You will get on very well with them. Their farms barely make ends meet; they struggle with every feed bill, Keith's jeep and tractor are ancient, and he would have to have a lottery win to have them repaired. But they are happy, generous and caring neighbours. Morag and Eaden are the salt of the earth and would help anyone out, even if it was their last penny. Farming is a hard game now, if you don't have more than one string to your bow.

"I would imagine they will be here at about six-thirty to seven, to make sure they see Izzy before she goes to bed. They must have the folks up looking after their broods, or it would have been a mad house with all the kids. Don't worry, and just enjoy yourself. I better go and get started or the day will disappear, see you at elevenses?"

"Yes, err, yes, of course."

When Izzy and James went outside to do the chores, Kate loaded the dishwasher quickly, deciding she didn't want to look like a total townie. She had a good look in the freezer to see what she could find to heat up. She found another one of Lorna's own chilli's, some garlic bread, two large plate pies, labeled savory and sweet, and luckily she and James had stripped the meat off the turkey at Christmas and frozen it – Kate thought she would make a turkey curry and a large bowl of rice. That done, she went upstairs to find something suitable to wear.

Oh, now hang on, she thought. Do I wear something fancy or are these people going to come casual, as they are probably coming on a tractor and are farming people. Oh, decisions, decisions.

Kate decided on a pair of smart black trousers and a little black cardigan with tiny buttons down the front and three quarter sleeves, cropped at the waist, showing a fashionable amount of skin. She thought that would cover any eventuality, black always did.

Kate walked over to the barn and the sun was warm on her face. It was hard to believe how cold it could get with the change of the wind. She carried the flask and she had made some, what her grandmother always called, egg bread: it was beaten egg, which you spread all over the bread and then fried it; ketchup made it even more delicious, and it was a comfort food for Kate when she felt down, so she hoped James and Izzy would like it.

"Hi, come and get it. I hope you like this, it was my favorite food when I was sad, or down, about anything…"

"Oh, Kate, I hope you are not sad now? We are going to have a lovely party. And you will love Aunty Lorna and Aunty Morag, and Keith and Eaden are quite mad. Dad and they will talk all the time about farming."

James said, "Now that's … erm, totally true."

They laughed as James was about to lie but changed his mind, as he knew that Izzy would call him a fibber.

"Hey, you're not worried are you, about Lorna and Morag coming?"

"Well, I was kind of wondering how you were going to explain me to them…"

"Don't worry. We will just tell them you got separated from your skiing group in the bad weather."

"Oh Kate, this is lovely. You are the queen of elevenses, isn't she Dad?"

James agreed with a vigorous nod of the head, as he was busy eating at the time.

"De-licious!"

The day seemed to gather speed after elevenses, and soon they were dressing and Kate was preparing to meet visitors, for the first time since she had arrived.

To say she was apprehensive would have been a slight understatement. Kate had lingered over a hot shower and was able to wash her hair properly now, as James had removed the sutures from her wound a few days earlier, praising himself for the remarkable repair job he had accomplished. She dressed carefully and applied a little make up, just basically to cover the faint bruising, which was still visible around the side of the face and the eye area.

"Well, Kate Johnson, that's it, that's the best you have. Here goes nothing."

"Who are you talking to, Kate?"

Said Izzy, as she walked into Kate's bedroom, intending to ask how she looked.

"Oh, just myself. I'm just giving myself a talking to, which I often do when I am little nervous. Oh my! Don't you look absolutely gorgeous? Oh, you look like a real little princess! No, you look like a real cherub: with your gorgeous new dress, and your lovely white tights and your fantastic curly hair. It's a shame we aren't going to the theatre or somewhere even more special than just a party at home."

"Oh well, I don't go to theatres, or anything fancy. This is the fanciest I will ever go to. You will love our parties; we always have a lovely time. Honestly, Kate, you don't need to be nervous. I will be with you all the time. And you look beautiful, now that your eye has almost gone, if you know what I mean?" said Izzy, in all seriousness, not realizing what she had said, and Kate loved her for it.

"Here they come, I can see the lights," said Izzy excitedly, running to the back door to greet them.

James emerged from his bedroom at the precise moment that Kate left hers, and their eyes took in each others 'party dress' appearance.

"Wow, lady, what did you do with the ragamuffin who arrived here a few days before Christmas? You look gorgeous!"

"Well, ditto," Kate smiled and accepted the compliment gratefully, but saying in return, "I must say, I never dreamed that farmers scrubbed up like you. You've kept that well hidden."

James was dressed in cream coloured chinos and a coordinated polo neck sweater, covered by a tan tweed double vented jacket, and brown brogues. He looked every inch the country squire.

James put his hand behind Kate as they walked down the stairs together. Kate realized that she had seen James only as a farmer, she had never seen any other side to him. Oh, she knew, because he told her, that she was the only one who he had confided in about his previous life and his marriage. She knew of course that his parents were both solicitors, and, obviously, quite comfortably off. But what she didn't know was James the land owner; James the gentleman; was he a gentleman farmer? She didn't think so. He certainly worked as hard as any farmer Kate imagined, though to be fair she didn't actually know any other farmers. Well, she thought, this evening may prove to be more interesting and less scary than she had anticipated.

As they arrived at the back door just in time to see the arrival of a vehicle that could only be described as, what looked like, a 'golf buggy', James laughed and laughed, and shouted a cheerful greeting to Eaden: "You bought it then? It looks amazing! How does it perform? How did it manage the track, even though you had ploughed it?"

"Oh, they're off, can you believe it? You have not even introduced us to your guest, and you are talking farming vehicles," Morag said in a mild rebuke to James.

"I'm terribly sorry Morag. You're right, where are my manners?" As James kissed Morag and Lorna in turn, wishing them the compliments of the season, and shook Eaden and Keith's hands warmly.

By this time they were all standing inside the door. James said to Kate, "Kate, I would like you to meet my good friends and neighbours: Keith, Lorna, Morag and Eaden."

Kate shook their hands, feeling a little less intimidated, as they didn't appear to have horns and were all smiling pleasantly at her.

"Honoured guests," said James, slightly tongue in cheek, "this is Kate, my house guest since Christmas, since she had a slight accident and got separated from her skiing party."

While everyone was taking stock of each other, a little voice said from closer to the floor: "And I'm Isabella Wallace." Izzy greeted them with a deep curtsey, and everyone, without exception, burst out laughing. Don't you just love her? Thought Kate, of Izzy, with the perfect timing of an awkward moment.

"Come in, Come in, let me take your coats and get everyone a drink," said James, the perfect host, again surprising Kate at the ease in which he handled himself.

She must get it in to her head that this is no ordinary farmer she had encountered, which would be hard, as that's exactly what she thought he was. It was becoming obvious that James' neighbors were indeed good friends, however there was something else that Kate detected as an outsider: there was a respect for the fact that they were James tenants. This evening could prove to be a very interesting one, not simply what the neighbors thought of her, but how they thought of James.

"Hi Lorna, you are the fabulous cook – I have not only heard about your food, but I have eaten a great deal of it this week. If your food was sold in stores in Manchester it would go like a bomb."

Seeing Lorna's confused expression, Kate said, "Not a bomb, I mean, sell like greased lightning – it's fabulous. And packaged from shelf to table, or freezer to table, for all of us single working women out there, you would make a fortune. No, no, I'm not joking!" Kate confirmed, seeing Lorna's embarrassed expression about her simple home cooked meals.

"Oh, and Morag, I am so envious of your talent. James and Izzy gave me two of your wonderful pots: the window box one and a round one with bulbs in for Christmas. You must be pretty well known in the local craft fairs, and such. I'm sorry I hadn't heard of your work before, but I have now, and I will look out for it and start collecting. That type of craft goes like a ... oh, sorry. I was going to say bomb, but I mean like wild fire, in the city."

Lorna and Morag were totally smitten with this woman – whatever she said or did now, it would be ok with them. They were like putty in Kate's hands, and the thing was, Kate was totally unaware of it. She was just being Kate, completely honest and naturally complimentary.

"I'm Kate, and for my sins, I landed poor James and Izzy in a terrible position over Christmas. The weather was so bad that I could not leave for Manchester, where I live, and they have been stuck with me ever since."

When Lorna and Morag had gathered their wits about them, they said how lovely it was to meet her and that they hoped she was okay after her skiing accident. Kate was in the process of waving a hand to signal everything was fine, when James appeared and asked who would like what to drink. The moment of awkwardness, which could have arisen, was lost.

Lorna had brought a basket full of wonderful food, and all the women set about warming it through, while the men talked.

"Tractors, farm equipment, and cows – I told you, didn't I, Kate? I told you that that's what Uncle Eaden, Uncle Keith, and Dad would talk about."

The women turned for a moment to see all the men thoroughly enjoying talking about Eaden's latest acquisition. Kate heard James' laughing loudly, saying how he didn't believe it that Eaden had actually bought his funny little golf cart off the internet. Eaden said, in a puffed up way, that he begged his pardon, it was an 'all terrain farm vehicle'. They all laughed again, obviously having a great deal of fun at Eaden's expense, though Eaden did not appear to mind.

"Just you wait until you can't get your tractor to work, Keith. And you have to haul silage to the field – snow just fallen and not enough room in the jeep, you will be wishing you had one of them," said Eaden, "they hold four people or a bale of hay."

The women left the men to their discussions about farming, which they had taken upstairs to the internet to look at vehicles online.

"Men," said Lorna.

"Totally," said Morag.

"I told you so," said Izzy, and they all laughed at Izzy's grown up expression.

The women all sat chatting. The wine flowed and the food was wonderful, so much so that Kate was telling Lorna, seriously, that her job in the city was in business and finance, and to take her word for it, if she didn't already sell to city outlets, she should seriously think about it. She asked Lorna if she had a brand name for her ready meals or evening snacks. Lorna laughed at first, then realizing Kate was serious, she asked Kate if she really and truly thought her food would sell.

"Are you kidding? Business and finance is my forte. Take my word for it, you have a product and a half here, Lorna."

"But I wouldn't know how to go about it. Cooking is one thing, Kate, but labeling, brand names, selling, that's a whole other ball game. It's all right for you – you're used to this type of thing. Come to think of it, you're used to the city, but I'm not."

Lorna, if you seriously want to do this, I will help you. I will give you my email address and I will help you sort your brand name and your market … actually, your brand name is best coming from you, because it should be something personal to you and Keith. It could be either the name of your farm or a combination of your names. Or, for example: Lorna's farm fresh cuisine, or something along those lines. But will it sell? Does a fish swim?"

"Morag, where do you sell your pottery?"

"Erm, well, I don't. I make it as a hobby."

"You're kidding me?"

"But Morag, it's absolutely fabulous! I'm not joking – shops in Manchester sell similar things for … well, take for instance the oblong window box container, with that type of glaze and decoration on, you would probably pay, erm, eighty pounds or so…"

Morag's sharp intake of breath indicated her disbelief.

"I'm not kidding you, Morag. And for the smaller one you would probably pay, err, possibly fifty pounds. And you're not selling them?"

"Well, I only make them and give them to friends. James often buys some from me to give as gifts. Besides I depend on the school kiln, as I don't have a one of my own, so I can only fire when the pottery class is firing, and that limits the amount of pots I can make."

"If you had your own kiln, could you make more? Do you have the time, what with your farm and everything?|"

"Oh yes, once I've thrown the pots and collected enough to fill a kiln, they more or less cook themselves, so to speak, and I decorate them if and when I have the spare time."

"Do you enjoy doing it?"

"Oh, I love it! I often wish I had taken it up when I left school, you know, as a job somehow. But of course, when you are born on a farm and marry a farmer, then you become a farmer's wife and that's that. Oh, don't get me wrong, I love being a farmer's wife and wouldn't want to be anything else, but I would actually love to spend more time potting."

"Would you want to do it as a business? I mean, would Eaden object if you started a small business?"

"Object? You must be joking. He would be over the moon if we were able to diversify in some way. We have been wracking our brains to think of something that would supplement the income from simply cattle and sheep, but we are not a dairy farm so we can't do cheeses or ice cream. Lorna does turkeys, which are a lot of hard work, but it helps them a little, doesn't it Lorna?"

Kate poured each of them another glass of wine, and as they talked, they noticed Izzy walking from each of them, listening intently. Then suddenly she said, "Hey, if you are all going to have businesses, why can I not have a business selling my rare breed hens and eggs? I will be in full production shortly."

The silence that followed was momentary, before all three of them laughed and laughed, until their eyes ran. And Izzy, who was looking amazed at whatever she had said, setting off this torrent of amusement, started to laugh with them.

"Oh Izzy," Kate said, putting her arm around Izzy's little body and cuddling her as she laughed, "do you know you are a born entrepreneur? And you are totally right – why can you not have a business, just like Lorna and Morag."

Lorna and Morag were absolutely lit up with the idea of starting a business, then reality set in, and in that moment they suddenly realized that no business could get off the ground without capital. Kate could see that a light had gone out and she said, "What? What is it?"

"Oh, Kate, it's a brilliant idea," said Lorna first, "but Keith and I are on our uppers and cannot even afford to get the tractor mended, never mind spend money on starting a business."

Morag said the same. She could not ask the school to let her use the kiln more often than she did, and, really, to run a business properly, she would need a kiln of her own.

"It's a great idea and its not that we don't want to do it," they said, "don't think we really don't appreciate your advice, but we cannot afford it," they said in unison.

"Listen," said Kate to Morag. "Apart from a kiln to get you going, what would you need? Do you have a work space that you could use?"

"Oh yes, we have space. And power and water in the old barn."

"So are we talking, basically, the kiln?"

"Well, yes."

"And you, Lorna. What would you need to start off your food business?"

"Well, you said I would need a brand name, so that would entail labelling, and containers, and some sort of advertising, I suppose."

"Well, we are not talking about a fortune here. So, what would you say if I offered to buy into your individual businesses, for a small percentage, and offer you a loan to get you both started?"

"Oh Kate, we couldn't do that. We hardly know you, and you don't know us at all."

"But I know James, and he says you are his wonderful, generous, and very, very, helpful neighbors. Listen, I'm not offering a fortune here, this could all be achieved for a couple of thousand pounds. I know that sounds lot to you, and it is a lot of money, but I am a single woman, and I have a very, very good job with a very good salary. And I don't do anything with it. I don't produce anything and I don't make anything. It would be a chance for me to be part of a new business venture; no – two new business ventures. What do you say?"

"I say yes," said a little voice. "But why do you keep forgetting me?" Izzy said

"Because, my little cherub, your business should have no partners, because you do all the work, but you can certainly be part of the new business trio at Comraich. Do you all agree?"

Lorna looked at Morag with excitement in their eyes, saying to Kate, "Are you sure you won't forget us when you get back to the City?"

"Well, if that happened, which it would not happen in a million years, you would have my money and you would be able to run your businesses without me anyway. So, it's a win-win situation, but I assure you I will be part of this venture."

Then they all said yes in unison, Lorna, Morag and Izzy.

Kate said they should celebrate with another drink; they talked business and then equipment, until Morag said a second hand kiln would not be as costly as a new one, as they sell them on the internet for reasonably cheap.

"Ok, I think the men have had the internet long enough. Let's go and throw them off."

There was a lot of excited laughing and hurrying to be the first to actually say to the men that they had been on long enough and it was now the women's turn. It all smacked of telling children to share, and Izzy loved it.

Then they went up to the little computer room and all began to talk at once, saying that they needed to have the computer. Then Morag said, trying to be calm about their need, but excited to get on with it, "We need to be on the internet for a while. You must be finished by now; surely there are not enough machines for sale to keep you up here all this time?"

All three men were shocked at the barrage of women who suddenly appeared. Despite some uncertainty, they decided to allow themselves to be led by James, to withdraw gracefully and go down to have a drink. James was smiling the smile of someone who knew he had been right about Kate getting on well with Lorna and Morag, and Kate saw his smile and smiled back with a lift of her eyebrows, and in return he squeezed her elbow without anyone else noticing the slight but warm contact.

They sat at the computer until they had exhausted all the second hand kilns, and any other equipment they may need to get started. They also looked at the different types of food outlets, Delis, packaging, labels, and artwork for publicity, until they had exhausted themselves. But instead of tiring of the idea it had filled them to the brim with confidence, enough to go downstairs and tell the men about their new venture. But first they all agreed that the best person of the four women who deserved to do what she would like to do for the next hour was Izzy: she had been brilliant, 'inspired,' Lorna said, 'entreprenereurial,' said Morag, and an all round 'good egg,' pardon the pun, said Kate, and they all laughed and went downstairs.

"Izzy has first choice at what we all do. This is her night as well as ours." said Kate.

Then after a long pause, Izzy said, "I would like to play charades."

And everyone talked at once, telling different stories about their last game, until the game began. It went on for about an hour and a half until everyone had been on the floor laughing at some of the silly ones that Eaden and Keith came out with. Lorna and Morag were indeed brilliant, as Izzy had said they were, and James was clever as a box of monkeys. Izzy's were more often than not chicken or hen related, but still hugely funny when she did the actions. At last, James suggested to Izzy that she was tired, and Izzy did not deny it. James carried Izzy up the stairs and helped her into bed while the others all flopped on various chairs, a little exhausted as well.

James came down the stairs and said he didn't know how Izzy was going to sleep as she was so excited about the new business trio that she was now part of, but by the time she got undressed and into bed she was almost asleep, so whatever it was that excited her, it also knocked her out.

"So what is this business trio all about?" asked James.

"Well, I think the girls should tell you all, as their husbands do not even know yet."

Said Kate, pulling an uncertain face, the kind that hopes everything is going to be okay, and that she hoped she hadn't caused any trouble for anyone, as that was the last thing she wanted to do among such good friends.

The next hour was taken up with Lorna and Morag telling their excited ideas, then the fact that Kate was going to buy into the business with a percentage, which would give them the capital to get the equipment they needed to get started. The idea was bounced around the room by all of them back and forth with suggestions and ideas. Neither of the husbands said anything negative about the venture, in fact they were all for it, telling each other that farming today was hard and that they had to diversify and how better to do it. The banks wouldn't help you, so they would have to get on with it and help themselves.

James stood up and said, "As absorbing as this new and exciting venture is, I think we are about to enter a New Year, so who will be the first- foot this year? Kate would you like to be my first- foot?"

"Oh James, you don't want me to be your first- foot, I may not bring you very much luck. I haven't had a great deal o luck this year in my own life, and isn't it traditionally a man?"

"Yes, but this year will be a new start for all of us, and you are certainly dark and handsome, so you will you do very well?"

"Well, if you really want me to. Show me the door and give me the piece of coal, or what ever."

Everyone joined in saying 'oh, you need coal, whiskey, and black bun and shortbread.' The list went on and on and they were all laughing, saying that if she didn't get outside before the clock struck, they wouldn't get any luck at all. Seconds before the clock struck the first chime, Kate was pushed out into the cold night air, with what looked like a full moon lighting up the farm yard; well, it did to Kate, in fact it looked like a huge silver disk, so close you could touch it.

She shivered. Despite having been so warm inside it was bitter cold outside. Everything sparkled with sharp edges of hard frost. Then the door opened enough for her to hear the last chime on the radio and she burst into the warmth saying, "Happy New Year!"

Auld Lang Syne drifted across the airwaves and everyone was kissing each other and wishing each other the very, very best this year, with much more hope and belief for their future. James kissed Lorna and Morag on their cheek and shook Eaden and Keith's hands vigorously. But when it came to Kate, his lips touched hers for the briefest of moments, but this time she responded immediately and felt the warmth of his mouth on hers long enough to savor long after she had gone to bed.

"Happy Hogmanay, Kate!" said James, close to her ear so that she felt it was for her ears only.

As the men took their usual stance next to the food in the kitchen, the women sat in the lounge warm and comfortable. The pace of the evening had slowed down and they were more relaxed with each other. When Lorna asked Kate why she hadn't had very much luck this year, Morag looked over with interest.

Kate said that it wasn't business, so they could put their minds at rest in that regard. She said she had an aptitude for business, yet in her private life, she supposed that she didn't have what it took. She said that she thought she had it made before Christmas, and life was going to be wonderful. This year was going to be her new start. There was a long gap before Kate decided that, if these women were going to be her business partners, she could not start off their relationships with a lie.

She began the story of how she and Dominic worked in the city and had been together almost three years, and how this Christmas skiing holiday was going to be so much more when she found she was pregnant. She told them how she imagined it would be when she told him her wonderful surprise, while they were sat in front of a roaring fire in the romantic log cabin. Then she told them what actually happened and how he had turned into something she had never seen before. She told them how she found herself in the snow in the middle of nowhere, and if it hadn't been for Elsa, James and Izzy, she would have died out there. How they had looked after her and mended her physically and mentally. She realized that as she spoke the words they were true: that she was mended mentally and physically and she was ready to sort out her life once and for all. And there was no place in it for Dominic.

Lorna and Morag both in turn stood up and came over to where Kate was sitting and put their arms around her to comfort her.

"And the baby?" asked Morag.

Kate shook her head and swallowed hard, determined not to cry.

Lorna and Morag both expressed the same sentiments: that Dominic was a 'bastard' and she was too good for him, and that she was young, beautiful and clever. They reminded her how far she had come in business without a man. They said that this year would be the year for all of them, and all three laid a hand one on top of the other and made a pact that this year was going to be their year. They said they wanted to say something up front with Kate, and she hoped that she would not take offense, but this was important to all of them including their men folk.

"James is a wonderful man Kate. He was very hurt and broken when his wife left – Jennifer. We didn't know her very well as she didn't mix with many people, but James has been a wonderful father to Izzy and she is a lovely, well adjusted girl. We wouldn't want you to hurt them in any way."

Morag carried on where Lorna left off.

"We can see that he has affection for you. He is different tonight, not the same as he normally is. Oh, he is always well mannered, well bred, generous and courteous, it's not that. But he has a light in his eyes that has not been there for a long, long time. So please don't do anything to hurt him, all right, Kate?"

"I would never do that intentionally, I promise you that. In the short time I have known James and Izzy, I have grown very fond of them, and could never do anything that would hurt them. I can see that you care for him very much, and I know he appreciates you all, he has told me that many times since I arrived."

"Aye," said Morag, in a mock Scottish accent, to lighten the tone of the conversation, which had become very serious. "The Laird is good to us, isn't he Lorna?"

"Aye, he is that," replied Lorna, in the same accent.

And they all laughed together and the atmosphere was restored.

"Hey, women of the house," shouted Eaden and Keith. "Are we going now before the dawn chorus starts and it's not worth going to bed?"

They all yawned and made their way to the door together, hugging and kissing everyone one in turn, saying what a wonderful new year it had been. Then off they went in Eaden's golf buggy, singing *Auld Lang Syne* in terrible voice.

James had laid his arm around Kate's shoulders as they saw everyone off at the door. She could feel its warmth through her cardigan. They turned, looking into the kitchen, and both looked at the array of supper dishes and left over food on the large kitchen table, and for a split second they considered leaving it until morning. But for some reason they both had the same thought: that tidying away would delay their parting and give them time to be alone, something they had been in the habit of doing over the last ten days or so. It did not take them long to load the dishwasher and put all the left over food into the fridge. James took hold of Kate's hand and led her through to the living room and they flopped down together on the large sofa.

"Well, was I right or was I wrong that you would love my friends?"

"Oh, you were definitely right. They are the most friendly, hard-working, genuine people I have ever met. They are not at all like the city types I work and meet with all the time. You know, I had almost forgotten what real people were like. I told them by the way…"

Kate looked at James' face, gauging his reaction to her revelation.

"I knew you would, in your own time. I knew that once you had decided to go into business with them, you could not start your relationship on a lie."

"Now how did you get to be so smart?" Kate went to poke James in the ribs and he pulled her forward gently until she was almost lying on top of his sitting frame. He slowly brought his head closer to hers, giving her ample time to call a halt if she wished to. As she made no move to pull away, he moved the fraction it took to place his lips on hers. This time there was no hurry and neither of them seemingly wanting to pull back. James' kiss was unlike anything Kate had experienced before – firm but gentle. Kate's lips were willing and warm beneath his. Kate was not expecting the spiral of feelings, which seemed to start in the pit of her stomach and burst upwards and into her chest, making her tingle with excitement. Kate distinctly heard James moan as his kiss deepened for a split second before he withdrew his warm lips.

"Well, a happy new year to you, Kate Johnson," James said, his voice thick with emotion.

"I think we better get at least one hour of sleep before we get into something we need time to think about very seriously, and not just as the dawn chorus is about to sing."

James stood up, and taking hold of Kate's hand, he pulled her up from the sofa, drawing her very close to him. He kissed Kate on the forehead and said in a devilish voice, "Go from me you temptress. I am a mere mortal and have cows to feed in less than an hour."

And with that, the atmosphere of ease was restored from the heady heat of moments ago. They climbed the stairs to catch a little sleep before the chorus actually did start singing.

Chapter 15

Kate thought she would fall asleep at the first touch of the pillow given the lateness of hour, but instead she lay there reliving the last few moments of the night and the kiss between James and herself. The warm fuzzy feeling, which engulfed her, sustained her for a moment until reality reared its ugly head. She wanted to tell it to go away while she savored the warmth of James' arm on her shoulder as they said good night to their guests, and the new year kiss where he had whispered in her ear, loud enough only for her to hear, or the longer, more lingering kiss while they sat together on the sofa. But reality could not be stopped. It was like a splash of cold water, bringing Kate back to the real world and the problems she faced.

Kate knew that she was becoming fond of James. Oh, who was she kidding? She knew that she was falling for him in a big way. She shocked herself by actually allowing herself to think it unequivocally after such a short time.

And Izzy – oh, how could anyone not love Izzy? She was the most lovable creature, and Kate was fast becoming besotted with her. The problem was, of many, she loved them both, and also, which came as a shock to Kate, the townie, she loved the life. She loved the earthiness of it all, the entire day to day routine.

She had known nothing else but business and finance, and she had come to the realization that she was bored with it. Yes, she thought, I am bored with making money for other people, with just figures on a balance sheet. Not to make ends meet or to see something grow, not to make a better life for individuals, the money she dealt with, she didn't even know who owned it.

Kate tossed and turned, knowing that in a very few minutes, she would have to be getting up, and she hadn't even closed her eyes.

She breathed deeply, thinking it would clear her head enough to fall off to sleep for at least fifteen minutes, but no luck. All it did was set her mind thinking again.

She made a mental list of what she had to do. First, it began with how she must change her life. It must be more productive, because as it stood at the moment, it was boring and not in the least productive. Secondly, she must sort out her private life; Dominic she knew was a thing of the past. If this last ten days had taught her anything at all it was that Dominic was not and never would be the type of man she could love for the rest of her life, and she knew now that James was right about that. Thirdly, was the hardest decision she had to make, and that was she must go back to her life and see if this excursion into wonderland, was simply that, or was it what she really wanted. And to be fair to James, he had not apparently, according to Lorna and Morag, and Izzy for that matter, had a relationship since Jennifer left. Was he simply being a gentleman, or was he a man in need of a woman's company. She knew at that moment that she must give them both the chance to see what life would be like without each other's company.

This was going to be the hardest decision of her life. Kate knew that she would spend the day writing each of them a letter explaining why she must go back to her life. She would leave a cheque each for her interest in the new businesses for the girls. She would give them her email address, mobile number, and home address, so that they knew that she had not just abandoned them and that she was completely serious about the business investment. Their letters would be easy to write, but she knew that the hardest thing in the world was going to be the letters to James and Izzy.

How do you begin to tell the man who has saved your life, and brought you back from the brink of desolation, physically and mentally, that you are leaving? How would she tell Izzy how much she had come to mean to her in such a short time, and that she was not abandoning her, but that she needed time to sort her life out? She would tell her she would be back and also put her mobile number and home address in, telling Izzy that she would wait to hear from her.

Kate decided to get up and have a shower, as it was clear that she would never sleep now, and she had come to a decision: that she could not simply carry on staying here in an attempt to avoid facing her problems. Today she must do something positive. It was the beginning of a new year and this was her resolution, she told herself silently: to do something about her boring life and change it for the future.

Breakfast was a quiet meal, as both James and she were so tired they were simply going through the motions. Izzy was, as usual, full of beans. James and Kate grimaced at her loud and cheerful presence. However, once James and Izzy went out to the barn, Kate decided to prepare her exit. She was not sure how she was going to achieve her goal, but she must prepare to leave. This could possibly be tomorrow, even if she had to ask Morag or Lorna to take her to the nearest station.

Kate spent the morning writing letters of explanation, none of which were easy. At last, she did finish them and put them safely upstairs out of sight. She then packed her case and shut the lid, so nothing could be seen, if either James or Izzy came into the room. All she had to do now was to figure a way of how to get to the station, wherever that was.

Kate made a special effort when it came to elevenses, as she knew that this would be the last time for a very long time, if ever. She made pancakes and coffee and took them across to the barn.

"Oh, Kate, you are too much," Izzy said.

And James said in a warm voice, directly at Kate, "I second that."

Kate made special detour to Sapphire's stall, saying in a low secretive whisper, "Goodbye Sapphire. Hopefully not for long." And she kissed the horse's nose.

Supper was an easy dish as they had so many leftovers from the night before, which only needed heating up. They had a funny mixture of dishes which always seem better the day after for some reason, as Izzy noted, wisely.

When Izzy went upstairs to bed, Kate followed her up and sat on the bottom of her bed and said a special good night to her, kissing the little girl's head before she came out of the room with tears brimming her eyes. Before she went downstairs she gave herself a moment to pull herself together so James would not see anything amiss.

James and she seemed to sense that things between them had to be given time, as last night's kiss proved to both of them that it would be so easy to jump straight into a relationship. However, they both had things which needed a lot of consideration. For a start, James had Izzy. He could not just dive into a relationship with someone if there was no future in it. That had already happened to Izzy, and he would not allow that to happen again.

They both agreed that, since they had had no sleep the night before, it would be best if they went to bed early. It was a relief to both of them, giving them time to think and breathing space to get their head around their burgeoning feelings for each other.

After breakfast the following morning, the opportunity that Kate never imagined arrived at the back door, shouting, "Postie."

Kate was in the kitchen and went to open the door, and a little man in a postman's outfit said, "Good morning." At Kate's astonished look, he explained that he was the 'post bus driver', and he was going to Inverurie, if there was anything they needed delivered. When Kate explained why she was surprised: that they had not seen anyone for over ten days, as the snow had blocked the road, and she wondered how he had got to the farm.

"Oh, my vehicle is used to the snow and poor weather. It would take a lot to stop the mail bus," the postman said, in a very broad Scottish accent, the kind that comedians imitated, but this was for real.

Kate thought, if this is not a lot, what does he call a lot?

A sudden thought came to Kate, and she asked if she had heard right, did he say he was the post 'bus'? He confirmed that he was indeed and would take parcels or passengers. Kate asked if he could wait a few minutes, and she gave him a huge mug of coffee to keep him occupied while she dashed up the stairs and quickly got her things together. She went into Izzy's bedroom and put the note she had written the night before into the hands of the big yellow chicken, which was a nightdress case, and which sat on Izzy's pillow.

She went into James' room, which she realized was the first time she had actually crossed the threshold of this very masculine man's domain. The quilt, which had a dark green and gold cover on it, was hastily thrown over his metal framed bedstead. An array of large, chunky, cushions, of matching colours, were thrown on top. She assumed that his mother had chosen the masculine colours for him. A quick glance around the room showed it to have heavy pine furniture in keeping with the masculine feel of the room. A smell of something lovely came from the en suite shower room as James had hastily dressed this morning, and she recognized the scent as distinctly James; Hugo Boss, thought Kate absently, or Calvin Klein.

She tried hard to concentrate knowing that she would love to have explored further but aware that the postman was waiting. She hurried downstairs.

She went through the kitchen and into the boot room where Elsa was lying in her bed. Elsa was now so used to Kate that she didn't feel the need to follow her around, so if she was not in the barn with James, she simply lay in her bed, quite content. This was distinctly unlike when Kate first arrived and Elsa thought it was her personal duty to take care of Kate every moment of the day. Kate knelt down to Elsa and hugged her huge head, scratching her ears. The tug of saying goodbye to Elsa was strong, as she felt that Elsa was her very own protector who had saved her life, in more ways than one. Kate sniffed in the tears and said in a snuffly voice to Elsa, "Don't forget me Elsa, I will be back. I promise."

And with that she said to the postman, "I'm ready. If you could take my pots, I will carry my case."

She had left both the envelopes for Lorna and Morag propped up in front of the phone, which had suddenly sprung into action over the New Year holiday. Kate got into the post bus, praying that neither James nor Izzy would come out of the barn at that precise moment, because this was breaking her heart and she could not face it head on.

Kate could not look back, and even if she did, she would not have been able to see anything as her eyes were brimming with tears. The little bus driver didn't seem to notice, as he chatted away to her about Christmas being over and it was back to normal, and he was looking forward to the spring now.

As they got to the end of the track, which led into Comraich, the postman got out to open the gate. Kate realized, at that moment, that this was the gate she had been leaning against that night. She could not stop herself from taking one last look. As she turned she could see the farm house with a plume of smoke coming out of the chimney, just like a cartoon drawing. In the distance she could see a very large house on the top of a hill.

"Who lives in that house, the one on the hill?" Kate asked the postman as he got back into the bus.

"Oh, that's Comraich manor house. Erm," he said, with a slight cough, "Well, actually, Mister Wallace and his wife used to live there, but they don't anymore. Erm, she left, I believe, and he now lives in the farm."

"Oh," said Kate, in a distant voice. She thanked him absently, as she came to terms with the fact that, when they talked of Comraich, it really was an estate, manor house, and all. James did mention the main house, but Kate never imagined it to be a manor house. And she did recall him saying that the farm manager had left, so he, effectively, was the farm manager, so naturally it was easier for him to be at the farm.

Chapter 16

The journey seemed endless, until at last Kate arrived back at her apartment in Manchester, and with the help and a very healthy tip the taxi driver helped her up with her very heavy pots while she carried her suitcase. He thanked her and got back into the lift. As Kate opened the door to the apartment and walked back into what, before Christmas, had been her whole life. She took a fresh look at the apartment with different eyes and saw a very sterile room with no atmosphere at all. There were no personal adornments, no children's pictures or toys, no haphazard lists of jobs to be done that day, and no overriding feeling of warmth. The apartment was cold and damp.

Kate sat down on her very posh and expensive white, Egyptian cotton covered sofa, and wept. She cried until it seemed that her lungs hurt. She had wanted to do that since the morning but had managed to hold it together until the minute she saw her soulless life spread out in front of her.

****

For the next few weeks Kate went through the motions of her job. She had received emails from both Lorna and Morag asking for her advice. They both seemed to respect the fact that, for whatever reason, Kate had left the way she had, and they did not pry. They both thanked her for the cash drafts she had left, arguing that they would never need as much as she had given; however, it was kind of her to think of them, when she obviously had a lot on her mind.

Helping Lorna source the information that she would need to sell her farm to home cuisine, and finding outlets and delis by asking if they would be interested in Lorna's food, gave Kate something to do to keep her mind off how terribly unhappy she was. She was in constant touch with both Morag and Lorna, but neither of them touched on the subject of James or Izzy and what effect her leaving had had on them.

Kate had placed the beautiful window box on her kitchen windowsill, and the hyacinths were on one of the benches in the corner of the kitchen, still with its little plastic wigwam on. Kate could see the beginnings of shoots coming through, so she would take it off soon, according to what Izzy had told her to do.

Kate tried not to think about Izzy as it hurt too much. She hoped that they hadn't felt betrayed. Kate was pained by the fact that she had left without telling them she was going, and she could not help but think it was just the same for James as it was when Jennifer had left. Would he feel relieved, as he did when Jennifer went, or did he miss Kate, as she missed him?

Weeks turned to months, and before Kate realized, March had arrived. It was still bitterly cold making it hard to believe that spring was on its way. She was in constant touch with Lorna and Morag and when she read their emails, which were full of business ideas and progress reports, she was proud of how they were managing their business without any previous experience. Lorna's emails were always full of gossip. She was thrilled to report that one of the delis that Kate had introduced her meals to had been in touch and put in an order for two dozen of her sample meals, since she had sent them a container of frozen samples for them to try. Oh, and by the way, Lorna had written, the farmers market cannot sell enough of my casseroles, it makes you wonder what has happened to home cooking if the wives are buying from the market, Lorna wrote. She didn't mind, though, it was all more sales for her. Lorna said, Morag has now got the stall next to hers on a Wednesday and Saturday, and Morag said to tell you she is selling everything she produces faster than it can cool down in the new kiln. Oh, and she also said to tell you she had had a letter from a very posh department store on Deansgate in Manchester, who have agreed to order a shipment of fifty window boxes as a trial. Lorna added that Morag thought she may have to stay up all night for the next week to fill the order.

Kate read Lorna's newsy email again and she could hardly see the keys in order to type a reply. Kate said she was thrilled with their progress and wished she could be there with them to be part of the excitement. Kate was desperate to ask about James and Izzy, and if she had only but known it, Lorna and Morag were both dying to tell Kate about them but never said a word.

The following day Kate received a call from a friend whom she had not seen for a while asking her to go out for a drink, as she had some startling news she might like to hear about Dominic. Kate agreed reluctantly, as she had not been across the doors since returning to Manchester. When she arrived home from Comraich, the first thing Kate had done, after charging her mobile phone, was to delete the dozens of texts messages and unanswered calls from her phone, most of which were from Dominic. At first she had toyed with the idea of actually changing her phone and not keeping her number, but that seemed a bit drastic, and after a few days at home with her phone charged but nothing from Dominic, she didn't bother changing it.

Meeting Gale, who had often accompanied Kate and Dominic, and a guy from Dom's bank, making it a foursome, was a little awkward, as it was obvious that everyone knew that she and Dominic were not together anymore. They had probably had some sort of story from Dominic so that he did not lose face, making conversation a little stilted between Kate and Gale.

"So, how are you, Kate? I was sorry to hear that you and Dominic had parted after a tiff on your romantic weekend in bonny Scotland."

"Oh, you know, I'm fine. I've just been a little busy since I got back."

"So have you heard about Dominic?"

"Heard what? I haven't heard anything. As I said, I have been really busy."

"Did you not know he has been suspended from work since Christmas? They rang him while he was on holiday, surely you knew that? It must have been when you two were at the hotel."

"Gale, I have no idea what you are talking about, he never said anything at all."

"Oh, wow. Well, apparently, he has been suspended from the bank – on charges of sexual harassment ... bullying a woman in his office. She filed a complaint about him, she alleges he hit her. Can you imagine that? Dominic, of all people. She must have fancied him and when he turned her down, well, you know what they say about a woman spurned and all that. I mean, I don't believe it for one minute. And I thought that I should tell you in case that was why you had broken up with him."

Gale waited expectantly for Kate to say that that was exactly what had happened, that they had rowed over the girl's accusation and they had parted on a tiff. Apparently, this is what Dominic had told everyone to explain Kate's absence.

"Well, erm, how can I put this, without sounding too melodramatic? Gale, six months ago I would have been shocked about that story, and you would never have needed to worry about me believing anything like that of Dominic. However, I'll tell you the true reason Dominic and I are not together…" And Kate began to relay her story to Gale, and somewhere deep inside, she knew this was going to cause trouble, but she knew somehow that this vacuum she had been living in these last couple of months was not normal: living in fear of bumping into

Dominic and not knowing what she would do or say, or meeting any of his friends from work and not knowing what he had told them, was constantly on her mind.

Gale said how shocked she was, and exclaimed, "And to think we had all been out together, who would ever have thought it?"

Gale was making all the right noises, yet Kate could sense an underlying disbelief from her. She knew that would be the general reaction from many of her and Dominic's friends, and who is to say that she was telling the truth rather than him?

The following evening Kate decided to order a pizza instead of having a meal on the way home, as was her usual habit. She wanted simply to get back to her apartment and basically wallow in her unhappiness, knowing however that she must eat. She put a twenty pound note on the bench, and just at that moment, hearing the door buzzer, Kate went to the door thinking it was the pizza delivery. She checked the video entry monitor: to her absolute horror, she could see Dominic standing there.

"Kate. Kate, I know you're there. I need to speak to you. Can I come up?"

After taking a deep breath, Kate knew that she could not ignore him or he would just keep buzzing. She said firmly, "We have nothing to talk about Dominic, please go."

Kate was shaking from head to foot. She had wondered what her reaction would be if and when they eventually met again, and now she was terrified and just wanted him to go.

"Kate, open this door. I just want to talk to you. We have got to talk."

Dominic was trying to persuade Kate by speaking quietly, but his anger was bubbling under the surface. Kate could sense he was like a coiled spring, and she was never going to open the door to him.

"Please go away Dominic, we have nothing to talk about. There is nothing between us anymore. You made that very clear when you beat me up and left me for dead. Now go away or I will call the police."

After ten minutes of silence, Kate started to breath normally again, deciding that Dominic must have gone away eventually. Then she almost jumped out of her skin when the door bell chimed, Kate went to the door thinking it was her pizza delivery and that she was just being silly. She opened the door.

But as she unlatched the door, the door swung in and hit her in the face with almost unbelievable force. Before she knew what was happening, Dominic was inside. He grabbed her face with one hand, and catching hold of her hair with the other, forced her head backwards. He spat his words out with venom.

"Who do you think you are, spreading filthy lies about me to all and sundry?"

"I didn't, Dominic. I swear the only person I told was Gale," Kate said through clenched teeth, as it was difficult to speak with Dominic's fingers squeezing her jaw.

"And who do you think she told, you stupid, stupid woman? She told everyone in the club, so now all my mates think I'm some sort of maniac."

Dominic's face was grey and his breath smelled of alcohol. His eyes were red as though he had not slept in ages, and he was acting like a man possessed. Kate truly thought if he killed her now he would not even know he had committed the crime when he sobered up.

"What did I ever do to you?" Dominic demanded of Kate, acting as though he were the innocent party.

"Women are all the same," he ranted. "They lead men on, then they complain if they get a little tap. This time," slurring his words, "you won't forget me."

Then Dominic said, with a menacing tone, he had come to rearrange her face permanently, and Kate thought she was going to faint, that this time there was no escape. Just at that precise moment the door bell chimed again, and the shock made Dominic lose his grip, and he let Kate go for a split second. It was enough time for Kate to run to the door and open it. Standing at the door, looking surprised at the speed with which the customer had got to the door, was the pizza delivery boy. Kate grabbed hold of his jacket and almost pulled him off his feet into the house. She said, as firmly as she could, as her insides were shaking and she felt as though she was about to throw up, "Well, goodbye Dominic, you will have to go now, my pizza is here."

Kate stood her ground. The pizza boy was looking from one to the other with a confused look on his face, but Kate hung on to his coat so that he could not escape before Dominic had left. In the end, Dominic would have to leave, or bodily throw the pizza boy out, who was no lightweight, or look totally stupid, standing there while Kate and the delivery boy looked on. Dominic eventually went towards the door, and as he turned and looked back, he said to Kate, "This is not over Kate. Don't think it is."

And he left, slamming the door behind him. Kate, still clinging to the delivery boy's coat, said to him, in a voice that sounded unreal to her, "Thank you, thank you – you will never know how grateful I am."

"You're very welcome, lady. That will be ten quid."

Kate grabbed the twenty pound note off the bench and said, "Keep the change, you deserve it."

The boy went off whistling. "Hey, thanks!" he called back, as she locked and bolted the front door behind him so fast he didn't even see her face.

Kate slid to the ground with her back to the door and cried a cry of self pity. It was the kind of cry that says: what have I done to deserve this? Kate could not move from the door. She was still scared. She didn't know how long she lay there before she eventually hauled herself up off the floor.

In the small lobby of Kate's apartment, she had a big heavy bookcase, the books on it making it even heavier. Kate tried to push it in front of the door, but it was too heavy. In her frantic effort to protect herself, she started pulling all the books off the shelf on to the floor, until eventually she managed to push the bookcase against the door. Not until she had the bookcase against the door did she feel safe. Kate walked to the sofa and slumped down. She grabbed hold of a cushion and pulled it to her body, attempting to comfort herself with something to hang on to. She lay down in the fetal position with the cushion jammed to her body and cried. She cried until she had no tears left. Eventually, she must have fallen asleep, because the next thing she knew, she could hear birdsong. It was still very early, as it was only barely light.

Kate dragged herself up and went toward the kitchen, feeling at least confident that the night was over and that Dominic had not come back.

Chapter 17

Kate made herself some strong black coffee and stood in the little kitchen with her eyes closed to the world, trying to restore some calm to her scattered thoughts. She could smell the most wonderful smell – hyacinth. She could smell the hyacinth and it was delicious. She opened her eyes and looked at the purple coloured blooms in the beautiful pot made by Morag and then at the window box, in which only yesterday two of her daffodils had opened up. As the morning sky started to get lighter, she stood watching her daffodils, and drinking in the smell of the hyacinths, until in an instant, Kate came to a decision.

"Why am I here? Why am I working at a job which I hate? Why am I not where I am happy and with people who care for me?"

Kate put her coffee down and dashed into the bedroom and started pulling suitcases out from the wardrobe, frantically opening and closing drawers, stuffing clothes in the cases.

Her heart began to sing because she was doing something she really wanted to do. In fact, it was all she had wanted to do since the day she left Comraich. She almost felt like laughing at nothing in particular, just excitement at leaving this flat and going where she would never be terrified again. Kate suddenly couldn't wait to leave her job, which she had spent all her time aspiring to move higher, and higher, in her profession – and for what?

It was becoming lighter now and she had packed everything she thought she might need, and this time it would include her bank book, her lap top, her mobile phone and charger. Last time she could not have phoned for help, even if she had been conscious, as her phone was in her flat. This time she would be prepared, as the boy scouts say, for any eventuality.

Kate still had the feeling that Dominic could be waiting, and she was terrified that he might catch her again, and this time she might not be so lucky. She decided to call a taxi, and she gave him her phone number, saying, when he arrived would he mind coming up to the flat for her, as she had heavy cases to carry. That's good thinking, Kate said to herself, almost hysterically, as her nerves became more and more stretched while waiting to hear from the taxi. Eventually the phone rang. She said hello, almost timidly, and when the taxi driver said he had arrived, she buzzed the outside door to let him inside. As he rang the door bell, Kate asked, through the intercom, who it was. The taxi driver probably thought she was a very nervous passenger, but nonetheless said who he was and she eventually opened the door. She thanked him and hurried down in the lift with him and into the taxi.

Kate would not breathe properly until she was in the train and on her way to Inverurie. As she stood on the platform, having been told she would have to wait almost an hour, Kate made sure she stayed with as many people as possible, feeling safer in a group. Kate felt as though she had waited for hours, but eventually the train arrived.

She managed to drag both her cases up into the train, with her laptop bag slung across her shoulder. She dumped both her cases on the rack inside the door. Then she took the first seat with a table in front of it – this she did from habit, as she would usually work during her journey in order not to waste a minute of company time. This time Kate would not be working, but she was going to try to send an email to Lorna or Morag, in the hope that one of them were on their computer.

She sent a brief email to each of them, telling them that she was on her way, and that circumstances meant that she had to leave Manchester in a hurry. She said that she was worried about how James would accept her, as she thought he must be really angry with her for leaving. He had not replied to her letter or rang, and what was worse, neither had Izzy.

To her amazement, within minutes of sending the email, she got a reply from Lorna, who happened to be online. Lorna said not to worry about a thing: at the moment it was lambing time and James could do with an extra pair of hands … and legs, come to that! She said, if Kate could make it as far as Tillynessle, which was the village outside Tillykerrie, she would wait for her.

Kate was jubilant. Oh god, she thought, how lucky that was, that Lorna be on line; oh, thank you god, I won't forget you for that, but I think you owed me a bit of luck anyway. After what seemed an age, Kate arrived at Tillynessle by taxi and saw Lorna's battered old jeep waiting outside the village shop. Kate paid the taxi driver before she got out and he jumped out and put her cases on the pavement, and thanked her for the very generous tip Kate had given him. Kate didn't even hear him, as she was occupied with hugging Lorna, the tears running down her cheeks totally unchecked.

"Oh, Lorna. You have no idea how much I have missed you, all of you!" Kate said, trying to gather herself and stop the tears, as she could hardly see. She searched for a tissue to blow her nose, and noticed that Lorna was in a similar state. They both laughed and sniffed at the same time.

Kate started first with a barrage of things she wanted to ask Lorna: "I have such a lot to tell you, and I want to know all about the business. But, first of all, how do you think James will take it when I arrive? How do you think he will react? Oh, I know I'm expecting a lot, he hardly knows me, and I've treated him badly, leaving like that. But Lorna, I had to know – I had to find out how I felt about my life. Do you see?"

"Listen," said Lorna, "we all have loads to catch up on, and we will. But I am going to drop you off at Comraich – the first thing you must do is speak to James. Things are frantically busy at the moment, because on top of everything, it's lambing time. James is the kindest and most understanding man you could ever hope to meet, and I'm not just saying that because I am his tenant. He is a dear friend to us. He will understand, I promise you."

And with that the short journey to the farm was over and the time had come to face James and hope he would give her a chance to explain. Lorna smiled and said to Kate that everything would be fine, take her word for it. And with that she roared away in the noisy old jeep.

Kate opened the familiar back door and dumped her cases on the floor of the boot room, where Elsa was in her basket. Elsa lifted her head, then she jumped out of her bed, and the loving dog made such noises of excitement that Kate thought James would be through before she had a chance to release herself from the over-excited dog. However, James did not come through, though a voice from the living room shouted, "Come in. Come in, whoever you are."

As Kate walked slowly into the living room, her heart pounding with excitement and anticipation, she saw James sitting in his chair opposite her. He looked up at her, his face a picture of complete shock, and she looked down at him in utter amazement. James was sitting in his chair with one of his legs propped up on a stool, and it had a plaster cast from toe to thigh. He had on a torn pair of trousers to accommodate the plaster and a thick sock stuck on the ends of his toes.

"Oh my god James, what happened to you? Oh, James. I'm so sorry for leaving the way I did. I couldn't think of another way to do it, and I knew I was becoming very, very, fond of you all, and I had to make the break sooner or later. Oh, James, I'm so sorry. I hope you can forgive me, and, oh my God, what happened to you? Are you all right? How did it happen?"

"If you give me a moment I will explain how it happened. And yes, I understand why you had to leave, and we, I mean I, well, I mean both Izzy and I, were becoming very dependant on you, I know. I hope we didn't treat you like a housekeeper.

"Oh, Kate. I am so glad you're back! You are back, aren't you? I wanted to come to Manchester and ask if you were happy, but then I thought, how can I do that? You were probably happy to be back to your job and your life. Then I broke my leg, so I would not let Izzy speak to you on the phone, in case she let the cat out of the bag and you came back because you felt sorry for us."

"I must go and say hello to Izzy. I have missed her so much. I was desperate to speak to her on the phone, but, like you, I thought that maybe you were not allowing her to speak to me, in case it upset her, the fact that I was just a voice in the distance. I was so worried that you would think of me as the same as Jennifer, and that is not how I feel James. I did not leave here because of the isolation. In fact the exact opposite happened: I feel so at home here."

When James gave Kate a puzzled look she was distracted for a moment, thinking about his face, his beautiful face, with his chiseled good looks, his dark hair and his piercing blue eyes. Kate thought she must concentrate and continued to say to James, "Isolation is a state of mind. I know that now because I have never felt as isolated as I did when I was in Manchester away from you. All of you: Izzy and Lorna and Morag and their wonderful hard-working husbands. If it hadn't of been for Lorna's gossipy emails, I would have gone mad."

James stretched out his hand and took hold of Kate's, squeezing it, "We have so much to talk about. I think we will need a crate of wine and months of evenings by the fire, but if you give me a hand up, we can go and give Izzy the surprise of her life. She has been fantastic. If it hadn't been for my wonderful neighbors and Izzy, I don't know what would have happened. I would have had to try to hire some temporary workers. They've forecast more snow, a lot more in the next few weeks. Oh, maybe not so deep, but at lambing time the last thing you need is snow and a broken leg. I need to be mobile. I need … well, I certainly don't need to be laid up and useless."

"Anyway, let's go to the barn and see Izzy, shall we? Kate helped James up from the seat, putting her arm under his and around his slim waist. He had a pair of crutches, which he obviously hated, but knew he had to use them. He had obviously been practicing with them, because he had become quite adept.

They went out to the barn, and between them, pushed open the door. James shouted, "Izzy," and Izzy's voice rang out from one of the stalls.

The first thing that Kate noticed was, instead of the empty stalls, which had been there when she left, all of the stalls were in use, and there was an amazing amount of bleating, coming from what seemed to be dozens, if not hundreds of sheep. The noise was so loud she was amazed that Izzy had heard James call. Izzy came out of one of the stalls, starting to say that the ewe was busy having twins and that it had started just after Keith had left. Then her little face lit up – there is no other way to describe it.

Her face shone like a little beam and she ran up the barn and threw herself bodily at Kate.

"Oh Kate, you came back! Oh Kate, we have missed you. Dad wouldn't let me talk to you on the phone, because he said I would tell you about his leg and you would feel sorry for us, and come back because of that. He said it wasn't fair because you have your own life. Oh Kate, I really, really wanted to speak to you and I really have missed you. Why did you go? Is it because we worked you so hard, with the cooking and all?"

"Oh no, my little Izzy. No, no – I love cooking for you and I missed making elevenses for you both, and getting all the compliments from the two of you. Do you know I have not cooked a meal since I was here?"

"Oh, you poor thing! Did you eat in those posh places all the time all on your own?"

"Well, yes I did. And I was so lonely without you. Listen, you need to get back to the sheep and I am going to change and come and help you, and I will tell you everything that's happened and how much I've missed you, okay?"

James said, no. She could not do anything as she had not come to work. But Kate said, then if she had not come to work, she didn't want to be here, because that's what she loved about Comraich: the feeling of being needed and actually doing something that makes a difference. James agreed and he said he would keep an eye on the ewe that was lambing while Izzy ran off with Kate so she could get changed.

Izzy and Kate talked almost as fast as Kate changed and ran quickly back downstairs. Kate said to wait a moment and she would make a flask and something to eat, because it may take longer than they thought. Izzy said Kate's elevenses was one of the things they both missed the most, then she said, but we missed you more, and Kate laughed, saying she knew what Izzy meant.

When they got back into the barn James was sitting with the ewe, wiping a new born lamb off in the straw while the mother licked the other two.

"Another triplet birth, Izzy, would you believe it? She scanned for two and out popped the third while I was looking the other way."

Kate was absolutely bristling with the sheer thrill of seeing new born life so close. She hadn't even seen life so young on television. Izzy explained, very knowledgably, "As soon as she has licked them we can spray their numbers on, so we know whose lamb belongs to whom, and then they can go in a stall of their own. Well, not a whole stall, we separate them with bails of hay and make them a lovely little warm, dry place, where the mothers can get to know their lambs."

Kate sat on a bail of straw in the barn and poured each of them a coffee, and as they all perched on the stacked bails eating their snack and drinking their coffee, for a moment neither of them spoke. Then all of a sudden they all wanted to speak. They laughed, and then James said, "We really missed this, didn't we Izzy? You bringing us our elevenses and us all sitting around chatting."

"Oh, you will never know how much I missed being here to make it for you. When coffee time came at work, I hated to even stop because the memory was so painful. And in an office, business carries on even through the coffee break."

"Well I hate to be a slave driver, but I have an awful feeling we are needed over there," James indicated a ewe in the corner, which seem to be circling around and around and making very threatening noises.

"What can I do?" asked Kate. "I want to be helpful. I do not want to be the city girl, so please show me. Throw me in at the deep end," she said, "I mean it."

So in at the deep end she was thrown. After about ten ewes were delivered and numbered and put into little stalls of their own, Keith came into the barn with a big smile on his face.

"Oh great, you've hired some new boy to help out!"

"Boy! You cheeky devil…" said Kate, who obviously hadn't seen herself for the last hour or two. She had put on one of James' heavy outdoor coats and a hat given to him one Christmas by his mother. Once again, it was one of his mothers' keep warm presents, but there was no way he was going to wear it, so he persuaded Kate to put it on, as she was not used to the constant cold in the barns. The hat was the type the Russian soldiers wore, and it had ear flaps like deputy dog, the cartoon. James wanted to laugh his head off but he was afraid Kate would not wear it if he did.

Actually, he felt like laughing at anything at the moment, he was so happy: happy even with his broken leg, happy even though he was frustrated at not being able to be active at the busiest time of the year; he was still happy and he knew why – because Kate was back. His heart was bursting he was so happy.

"Hello, Keith. It's lovely to see you again. I can assure you I am not a boy. I hope everything is going well at your farm, and with Lorna and the business?"

"Business? Business? I'll give you business…" said Keith, in mock annoyance. "We have never stopped – we are working flat out: lambing, farming, helping out the lord of the manor here, and now this blinking business. She can not cook it as fast as she can sell it. And who has to deliver a constant supply to the train? I'll give you two guesses…"

Keith leaned over to Kate, who was not quite sure what he was going to do. Suddenly, he grabbed a manhold on her and plonked a kiss on her cheek, saying how lovely it was to have her back, and that he hoped she was here to stay this time, and how the business was making a small fortune. The only problem was they needed four pairs of hands each to cope with the demand.

"Go on you lot. Go and have a little rest and I'll do the next few hours, but then I must get back to my place to give Lorna a break. She has orders to fill for first thing in the morning. Things should get a little easier though, now that the two main customers in Manchester have got together and arranged for food to be collected by van. Apparently they have a few businesses up this way, so it suits them to have their food collected fresh from the farm."

Chapter 18

Kate and Izzy made their way out of the barn, making for the house, leaving James still talking to Keith. As Kate and Izzy walked away she thought she heard Keith say, "Didn't I tell you she'd be back? She cares, I told you so."

Then Izzy was talking and Kate didn't hear any more. The two girls chatted and giggled, and Kate said how she should be exhausted but she wasn't – everything was too exciting, as she had never delivered a lamb in her life, and now she had helped to deliver at least six since she had arrived.

My, thought Kate, was it only today that she had arrived? Was it only yesterday when Dominic… But no, she was not going to think about that and spoil her happiness.

Kate and Izzy dragged her cases upstairs, and while Kate put her clothes back into the chest of drawers, Izzy sat on the floor, telling Kate very sensibly that she was too dirty to sit on her bed. Kate bent down and sat on the floor next to Izzy for a moment. She took hold of Izzy's chubby little hand, telling her very seriously that it was the smell of the hyacinths, which Izzy had planted her for Christmas, that prompted her to come back to where she was the most happy, the happiest she had ever been in her life. Kate leaned over and cuddled Izzy, then looked at her and laughed.

"You are the dirtiest child I have ever kissed." And they laughed together, Izzy saying Kate wasn't so clean herself.

Kate cobbled together a meal from the freezer. Thank heaven for Lorna's cuisine meals, thought Kate. They all sat around the kitchen table and ate the hastily prepared meal, enjoying every mouthful. Kate said she would make some sandwiches for the late shift, and Izzy said one of the ewes, which had lambed, had rejected her lambs, and asked if her dad could make her some little coats out of the skins of the dead lambs. Kate looked up, a little horrified, but James explained that it was normal practice, and it helped to keep orphan lambs alive. They hope that another ewe with only one lamb will take an extra one on, or it means bottle feeding, and they simply didn't have the time or the people. Kate saw the logic in that, and then it suddenly came to her that she was sat at this table doing exactly what she had seen James and Izzy do. When she first arrived before Christmas, they discussed the business of running a farm, and now she was part of it. Suddenly, she was one of them. She could not have been happier if she had tried, she felt accepted.

"James, should you be doing as much as you are? What did the doctor tell you? To rest, I'll bet. You know, Izzy and I can manage for a little while. Why don't you make the little coats for the orphans and put your leg up and rest it for a while? We can manage, and if we can't, Izzy will come and get you."

"I'll do that, I promise. But from inside the barn, you cannot do it Kate. Now, don't get me wrong, you can do a lot, and I am really, really grateful for your help. It goes without me saying, but within seconds something can go wrong, and you would need me and it would take me tens minutes to get to the barn. All the hospital said was to keep the leg up as much as possible. Well, that's what I'm doing. Unfortunately, that's not as much as they would like, I know. I am not silly, I will do as you suggest. But I am better off in the barn with you than sat in the house."

James and Izzy went back to the barn while Kate cleared away the dishes, started making sandwiches for later, and filling flasks with hot coffee. Kate had never felt so needed or alive as she did at this moment. She had enough adrenalin to keep her going for a week. She had not felt like this for a very long time.

Back in the barn, the ewes seemed to be popping like corks. After three hours and at least twenty more lambs, Kate lay back against a bail of straw. During this temporary lull, she expressed to Izzy how strong she must be: "You have been at this all day, little girl. How are you not on your knees by now?"

Izzy laughed a tired laugh and said she was used to it. But James saw that Izzy was indeed tired. In fact she looked totally worn out.

"Izzy come and sit by me and have a sandwich and a drink. Then I think you should go to bed, my darling. You have worked your little socks off."

Izzy started to complain that she was fine, but in all honesty, she had to stifle a yawn, and even she knew that she needed her bed. She said she didn't think she could eat a thing and would just go straight to bed, but she would be up all the earlier in the morning, and she reminded them not to let her sleep in.

"It's absolutely wonderful that you are back, Kate" Izzy added, and came over to give her dad a goodnight kiss. Then she came to Kate and put her little arms around Kate's neck and kissed her cheek.

"Hey, nobody is happier than I to be back, and I will tell you all about it tomorrow when you get up. Do you need any help? You look awfully bushed to me."

Izzy said, no, she would manage. She said goodnight, then went off to bed. Kate said she would check on her when she next went into the house, in case she had fallen asleep on the carpet, to which they both laughed, saying, knowing Izzy that would be more than possible.

James was making little coats for the orphan lambs. Kate lifted the lambs to him while he fitted it over the lamb, rubbing all over it at the same time so that the mother would be fooled into thinking it was her dead lamb. It was all very common sense once you got round the idea of skinning a lamb, which Kate could not do to save her life. She was not hardened to that side of farming yet.

They worked steadily for another couple of hours until Kate said she would have to have something to eat. Her appetite, which had been missing for weeks, had come back with a vengeance. She dragged a bail over to where James was sitting and poured them out some coffee and opened the box with freshly made sandwiches in and sat back with the sigh of a manual worker who had stopped for a well-earned break.

As they sat in the barn, with all the extra temporary lights strung between the stalls, giving more light to where they were working, the light seemed to make the little compartments where the ewes had their new lambs much warmer than it had been earlier, and it felt quite cozy. James and Kate were exhausted, but still enjoying their break. James smiled and moved to rub Kate's dirty face, but as he did she winced. James pulled back, surprised.

"Are you okay? What is it? Did I hurt you?"

James took a closer look at Kate's face and saw that it was not dirt on her face – one side of her face was darker than the other. He hadn't noticed before because he thought she had been rubbing her face while she was working. But this was not dirt.

"Kate?"

Kate took a deep breath and a looked round at the lambing shed, and it did not look as though any ewes were imminent at present, so she started to tell James what had occurred. She started by telling him how she knew the minute she had got back that it was the wrong thing, but that she had to do it to make sure; however, she could not tell him all: about how she had missed him so much she had cried herself to sleep. How could she? She did not know how he felt about her: was it all too premature? Was all the interest on her side? She didn't think so, but how could she be sure. She told him that, when she charged her phone when she had got back from Comraich, Dominic had left her message after message. He must have given up eventually, when he had got no reply.

"Or," said James, "he thought you died out there in the snow."

Kate said that during January and February she never heard a thing. She didn't hear a word about Dominic until she met a friend for a drink, at her friend's insistence, as she wanted to tell Kate the scandalous news about her ex, and hoped that wasn't the reason they had broken up.

Kate said it the way Gale had meant it, which was that Gale just wanted to know the inside story of Kate and Dominic's break up, so she could pass it around. Knowing that, she should have guessed that she would pass on what Kate told her about the 'so called tiff', which Dominic and they were supposed to have had, which had caused the break up.

Kate said, maybe she did want Dominic to know; she wasn't sure anymore.

"All I know is that it felt as though I were waiting for the hammer to drop, and living in a state of nothingness. I wanted it to be over one way or the other. I could never have imagined how it would happen and how scared I would be."

Kate described the look on Dominic's face as he threatened her, with his fingers in a vice-like grip on her jaw, and his other hand grabbing her hair tight so that she could not move or help herself. How he threatened to 'rearrange her face permanently this time'.

"Oh god, James. I was so lucky that I did not eat out that night, but decided to order a pizza, instead. Don't let anyone tell you pizzas are bad for you, because this one was to die for."

James quite rightly looked puzzled, and Kate said sorry, and got back to her tale of what happened when the door chimed again, and Dominic was taken off guard for a split second, just long enough for Kate to make a run for the door.

"That poor delivery boy, I almost pulled his arm out of his socket. I never let go of his coat – he will never know how close he came to saving my life; he must have thought we were just a couple having an argument. When I tipped him he was thrilled to bits."

Kate took a deep breath and told James how she had pulled the bookcase in front of the door until the next morning and lay on the sofa until it was light. She even told him about the smell of the hyacinth, and the daffodils, and how at that precise moment she knew that she had to get back to Comraich as fast as her legs would carry her. She told him how she was sure that Dominic was still out there and how she had made the taxi driver come up to the apartment so they could go down to the car together. And about the train journey back and how she had been so relieved when in answer to her email Lorna had collected her in the old clapped out jeep.

James let out the longest sigh, shaking his head. At first he seemed to be at a loss for words. Then he said to Kate, "Why in God's name didn't you ring me? We thought, Izzy and me, that you were back to your life and didn't need us anymore. We really, really, missed you Kate. Then, when I broke my leg, I thought it would look like we rang you because we needed you. And all the time you were as unhappy as we were."

James couldn't tell Kate how desolate he had felt when he had found her letter. That his mind had not been on his work for weeks after, and it was because he wasn't concentrating he had made such an elementary mistake and broke his leg. How could he tell her that he missed her so much? That he and Izzy had began to feel as though she were family, and when she went away neither of them could stop thinking about her?

James was incensed with this despicable pretence of a man. He wanted to get his hands on him, ring his neck, call the police and have him charged with assault, or grievous bodily harm or what ever it is. But Kate said that would mean taking him to court, which would involve seeing him again. The thought of seeing Dominic again scared Kate so much that she reached over to James and grabbed hold of his arm to plead with him to let it go, saying she felt safe here, and she was scared he would find her. James put his arms around Kate's trembling body and hushed her, saying, "No one is going to make you do anything you don't want to do." He promised her this, rocking her to and fro, gently comforting her.

James kissed the top of Kate's head. His face was a picture of barely concealed anger and frustration, because he had been unable to help Kate when she needed him most. Over the years, since he came back from overseas, James had tried hard to control his feelings of frustration and impotency at not being able to help in situations that were beyond his control. James knew that it had taken him over seven years to come to terms with his anger and frustration of some of the sights he had seen. He wondered, though, how he would react if he came face to face with the man who had hurt Kate. Kate was so terrified, and he so angry, that if they let it, this thing could spiral out of control and hurt each and every one of them. No, Kate was right. But they had to do *something*, if only for the young woman who was involved in the suspension at the bank.

"Kate, I agree not to do anything that will involve you having to see, or speak, to Dominic again, but can I make a suggestion? Will you listen to what I have to say? Before you answer?"

Kate knew that whatever it was, James would not let anything happen to her. She nodded her head and agreed to listen to his suggestion before making a decision.

"If you don't want to do anything about your own situation with Dominic, I understand why, so don't get worried that I am going to try and persuade you. But what about writing a letter detailing your account of the incident, and sending it to the person who is dealing with the young woman's sexual harassment case. If you don't tell them about Dominic's character, it is her word against his, but with your evidence behind her she would win, and he would get his comeuppance, without you even having to be there.

"Oh James, that's a brilliant idea. I feel that, somewhere deep inside, I should feel sorry for the person I once thought would be the father of my child, and my husband. But all I can think is: what happens if he finds me again, and finishes what he started? Even worse: what happens if he does it to some other girl? No,

271

you're right, James. I will do it." Kate turned her face up towards James, and said these words with her eyes full of something very warm for this wonderful man. She felt a great weight off her shoulders, and he had done it.

"You have no idea. I will sleep for a week, and it has nothing to do with lambing until the early hours of the morning," and Kate's words trailed away as she was looking into James' dark eyes.

Kate's lips were still parted when James's firm mouth covered hers. They twisted closer so that their bodies could touch. They grasped at each others heavy clothing, trying to hold on to the firm shapes beneath. Excitement rising and breath coming in short gasps, it took a while before either of them could take in the heavy grating of the barn door being pushed open, and a voice calling.

"Hello, Hello! Little Bo Peep, who is tending the flock tonight?"

It was Kate who got her voice back first and she managed to shout in a breathless tone: "Hello, hello, I am Little Bo Peep. Are you the big bad wolf?"

And as the voice came closer then suddenly showed its face above the stall. It was Eaden. He took one look at the two of them and said, "I think the wolf is already here, my dear. I would be very careful."

They all laughed and Kate said how she could not get over a neighbour coming at four-thirty in the morning to help out. She had never known anything like 'country folk' for being so kind and generous, and as she said that, her glance went to James, and James' face went a dark colour, as Eaden noticed with his keen eye.

"Oh, it's not all country folk Kate. It's only us peasant farmers who are tied to the Laird," said Eaden tugging at his forelock.

They all had a laugh about that, knowing that James was the best landlord anyone could wish for.

"Hey, do I at least get some coffee before you good folks go to your beds?"

Kate said she would go and make some fresh coffee for him, but Eaden refused, saying he didn't mind what was left in the thermos, and if there were some sandwiches left he would eat them as well, if they were going. James and Kate said he was welcome and they would take the opportunity to go to bed now and thanked Eaden, who waved his hand with the gesture of 'what are friends for'.

James and Kate walked slowly back to the house. They dumped their dirty boots and coats and both agreed they were too tired to eat or drink and would go straight to bed. Kate waited for James, as he found it easier to mount the stairs on his behind. She bent to help him to his feet and he leaned over and kissed her once more. This was the fleeting kiss of goodnight, but enough to sustain both of them in their dreams.

Chapter 19

Kate felt as though she had just closed her eyes when she heard Izzy shout down the stairs to her father, and then James shouted back, in a type of stage whisper.

"Shush … Kate is still asleep. We didn't get a lot of sleep last night, or should I say, this morning. You seem bright as a button as usual; it couldn't have something to do with having Kate back, could it?" said James in a jovial and conspiratorial voice, knowing that Izzy knew he was just as happy as her, but just not hopping up and down, which would be hard to do in his cast. James started to cook breakfast as best he could, with Izzy doing all the fetching and carrying, and James leaning against the Aga, cooking bacon and eggs, his broken leg resting on top of a stool. Between the two of them they made a pretty good team, Kate thought, as she stood at the kitchen door without saying a word, just watching father and daughter working together. Both of them must be very tired, and yet they still had time to joke and laugh. In fact, Izzy was trying to put a sock onto James' foot with the plaster on, and tickling his toes at the same time.

James was saying, in a mock serious voice, "Now, now. Stop that you devil, or you will not have any breakfast."

"I hope there is some breakfast for me, because I am starving."

"Oh, I'm sorry. Did we wake you up? We were trying to be quiet and give you a little lie in bed."

"I heard."

Kate said in a mocking voice, "No, no, I want to be up. I wanted to make breakfast for you both; I have looked forward to it ever since I went away. You know, when I'm at my apartment, I don't have breakfast, I have a cup of coffee on the way into the office.

"You mean while you're driving?" Izzy said in amazement.

"Oh no, I gave my car up a couple of years ago now. I walk or take a taxi, it's quicker.

It's not worth having a car in the city, nowhere to park."

"So how do you have your coffee on the way to work?"

"Well, in the city, there are street vendors selling coffee, bagels, muffins, you know?"

It was clear by both James' and Izzy's face that they would not like that. James of course had seen all the street vendors in Asia and India, so it was not new to him, but Izzy thought drinking your coffee on your way to work was unnatural, and she was right: since when had life become so fast that sitting down and having breakfast at home made you feel as though you were time wasting? Not having a car simply because it would take extra time to park, not going home in the evening and cooking a meal but eating on the way home instead, to save time. Kate could see so many things, which seemed normal to her only a few months ago, that now seemed ridiculous. She wondered when the world had become so Americanized.

"From now on I am going to start my day with breakfast, sat at the table with my favorite people, and that is most definitely the two of you," Kate finished with a bright, feel good smile, and put her arms around Izzy's little body, squeezing her gently, saying they would never know how much she had missed them both. Having breakfast with them, chatting about the farm, she knew to them it was all perfectly normal, but for her it was like being part of a family, and Kate loved it.

"Izzy and I vote that you never go away again, and that we are your surrogate family. Don't we, Izzy?"

"Oh yes, yes."

Lambing was a hectic, tiring, but wonderful time. Not only seeing all that new life, which Kate thought no one could ever tire of, but everything about it. James and Kate worked side by side, and Izzy objected strongly, for the first time in her young life, to going to school, claiming she was needed more at home at a time like this. For such a young child she gave a good argument, however she was voted down by the joint court of James and Kate, telling her she would appreciate, one day, being made to go to school. Izzy was not convinced.

On Saturday morning Izzy was up early. James had said at dinner the night before that most of the ewes and lambs in the big barn could now go out into the field as the snow had almost gone, though because of the height of the farm they still had heavy snow flurries. But most of the lambs were healthy enough to withstand the chill and they were better off in the field with the rest. The plan today was to shuttle ewes and lambs in the trailer on the back of the quad. If James was frustrated when lambing started, he was almost beside himself now: normally he would simply have done trips back and forward to the field, dropping trailer loads of sheep and lambs; however, he could not drive the quad, and that left only Izzy. And although Izzy was experienced, James still liked to be there with her, in case any of the ewes got a bit nervous that her lambs were being taken away.

"Why can Kate not drive the quad dad?"

This made perfect sense to Izzy: if Kate could drive a car then why could she not drive the quad?

"Because Kate has never driven one before, Izzy. And it's not that easy, they are dangerous."

"Well, if Izzy can ride one, surely I could manage, if you showed me how?"

James mumbled under his breath, saying it was not that easy, that Izzy had been on a farm since she was born and Kate could get injured, and so on.

"Well, surely you could just try me? See how I do. And if I am a total dodo, then I promise not to press you." Said Kate, glancing at Izzy and winking slightly, without James spotting them conspiring. James should have known never to take on two determined women. It was obvious that he was out of practice and did not notice the way they had manouvered him into agreeing to let Kate try.

James agreed, but only if Kate would wear a safety helmet and a thick coat, in case she was to come off. Kate stopped him, saying that she would not be able to ride the quad if she was so bundled up with clothes. James agreed reluctantly, mumbling all the time about how this wouldn't have needed to happen if he hadn't of broken his stupid leg.

Kate sat on the bike while James gave her instructions, saying over and over that there was no hurry and not to go too fast. As she ran the bike up and down the farm yard, Kate had never felt so exhilarated, and was thoroughly enjoying herself. Every time she started to go a little faster, James would say to slow down. Eventually, James agreed that Kate could do a trial run, as long as she was very, very careful.

The trailer was hooked up, and between the three of them, and Tip, they managed to round up the ewes and lambs into the box. James was hobbling on his crutches, using one crutch as a crook, and giving instructions to Kate, telling her to drive very slowly as it would feel different with the trailer on the back. Tip was in the trailer with the ewes, who were making a terrible racket. Kate hoped that that was normal and it wasn't her driving upsetting them. Kate found herself shouting to make her voice heard over the noise of the quad, saying that it wouldn't be long, they were almost there and she would let them out with their babies. It would have been obvious to anyone listening that she was not a famer's wife and that eventually she would not even notice the noise, let alone talk to the sheep.

Getting to the field was easy enough. It was within sight of the main house, and there was only one track leading to it. Opening the trailer and letting out the anxious mothers and lambs was another matter; however, Tip knew exactly what to do, and within minutes of taking the bolt out of the tailgate of the trailer, the sheep and lambs jumped out and Tip was herding them up the field.

Kate felt absolutely thrilled with her achievement. She was ready to race back and collect more sheep. The wind whipped past her face, which she knew without seeing in any mirror, would be bright pink from the biting cold air. None of this bothered Kate. She had never been so happy and full of life. Kate arrived back in the yard, where James was still standing in the bitter cold, watching her every move.

She told him quite firmly that he should go inside and rest his leg; she and Izzy, not to mention Tip, who was a person all on his own, would manage, and they would be finished in no time.

"Please, James. Your plaster comes off next week you don't want to cause any problems with your leg. And you are not able to keep as warm as we are, because you can not move around quickly. Please, James. We can manage, honestly. And I'm loving it, so you have no need to worry. And I promise I will be really, really careful, honestly."

"I can see you are enjoying it, that's what worries me. You are enjoying yourself too much. You are going too fast. Please be careful: I would never forgive myself if anything happened to you, Kate."

James took hold of Kate's hand as he spoke and gave it a squeeze. Izzy was loading up the next ewes and James thought that she hadn't seen what happened next. James leaned over and kissed Kate's cold lips, mouthing the words as the bike's engine was so loud, speaking normal was impossible: "Be careful," he said.

Kate nodded and gave a smile that melted James' heart, as he could see the pleasure she was gaining from simply helping him and doing something she was enjoying.

Between Kate, Izzy, and Tip – who Kate was not only not afraid of, but whom she admired tremendously, as he had worked tirelessly and seemed to know exactly where he was supposed to be, and where the sheep and lambs would run to – after two hours they had taken all the ewes and lambs that were capable of being out in the cold, and the only thing left to do now was take some bales of straw out into the field, to act as shelter in case of snow or rain. Kate and Izzy decided it was time to have something to eat and drink, and they suddenly realized how hungry they were.

When they went inside, the smell of food was delicious. It was clear that James had not been idle. They heard James on the shortwave, saying thank you to Keith, before coming through to serve dinner. Suddenly, everyone was talking at once. Kate was saying the food smelled divine, Izzy was saying that Kate drove the quad as though she had always ridden one, and James was telling them to sit down and he would put dinner out, with Izzy's help to carry it to the table of course. Kate said the only thing they hadn't done, but they would do it after dinner, was to take the bales to the field.

James said he had just spoken to Keith, and he was going to do it with the flat bed. It would save them both from having to do half a dozen trips. "So that's sorted, and you are both on official rest period now," said James firmly.

As they sat at the table eating and talking, Kate said that if her jaws didn't already know what to do without her helping them, she didn't think she could chew her food, even though it was delicious. Izzy laughed and laughed at that, saying how funny Kate was, and how she had done really well for a beginner on the quad.

"Do you know," said Kate, "I've always wondered what people get out of those *dude ranch holidays*. I've watched those holiday programme's, and they just made it look as though you pay a lot of money to work on somebody's farm, and do their work for them. I never saw the attraction before. But I do now. I would do it and pay for the pleasure. I have had such fun today. I am totally exhausted, but I have loved every single minute of it."

Kate's eyes were shining. Her face was rosy and her hair was a mess, but to James she looked, gorgeous. This woman was something else: beautiful, hard working, great with animals and kids, and she actually loved farming. James' had not realized, but his eyes were devouring Kate up, and he would not have been embarrassed if anyone had witnessed it. He knew that he was falling for this woman in a big way. That was the problem. He was out of touch. It was a long time since he had dated anyone. Would it be too soon? Would he be pushing it? How long do you wait for someone to get over a traumatic relationship like the one she was in?

Izzy went up to bed. She was a very grown up little girl in lots of ways, and knowing when she was tired without being told was one thing Izzy knew instinctively. Knowing, as well, when her dad and Kate needed time together on their own, was another of her talents, which neither James nor Kate realized.

Kate said she would go up and shower, then come back down and laze on the sofa. She stood up to collect dishes and James said, in a mock firm voice, "Kate Johnson, you are not the housekeeper, you are not clearing dishes after a full day on the farm. Anyway, you're my temporary sheep herder," and they all giggled.

Kate said goodnight to Izzy, after she had jumped into bed. "If I wait to say goodnight until I've had my shower, you will be fast asleep. I've never known anyone go to sleep faster than you."

Kate leaned over to Izzy and said, "Hey, thank you."

"What for?"

"For being my teacher, my helper, and my friend today. And for tricking your dad into letting me ride the quad. He doesn't even know we did it to him."

They both laughed, as people do who have done something not quite above board. Kate kissed Izzy on the cheek, and as Izzy lay down she said, "You're my best friend Kate, and I hope you never leave again."

"I'll do my very best cherub, I promise."

Kate had a hot shower, luxuriating in the heat of the water, easing her tired but satisfied body. She dressed into a pair of pale lemon pyjamas, which suited her almost olive skin. She wrapped a towel around her wet hair, and then went down stairs. She didn't know how James had managed to carry everything into the lounge, but he had brought coffee, cups, glasses, and a bottle of wine. The evening had turned dark, and the only light in the room were those of the table lamps. The fire, as usual, was burning bright, with the doors open to heat the room.

James was sat in the middle of the sofa with his broken leg resting on a stool and a cushion under his foot. Kate knelt down in front of the fire with her hair brush in hand and started to dry her hair with a towel before brushing it. It should dry fairly quickly in front of the fire, said Kate. James gestured for her to move closer, and before she knew what he was going to do, James started to rub Kate's hair dry with the towel. He removed the towel and beckoned for her to give him the brush, and he started to brush her hair. It should have felt strange, but it actually felt heavenly, as Kate was so bone tired, it was nice for someone else to pamper her for a change.

"So hop-a-long, how did you break your leg? You never did tell me?"

"Well, I was doing something terribly brave: saving someone's life. And I had an accident in the process."

"You rotten fibber. Come on, fess up."

James wondered for a moment if he should tell the actual reason: that simply because his mind was not on his work, and on Kate instead, he made a simple error.

"I was putting a heifer into the crush to give her an antibiotic, as she had had a particularly bad time calving. She didn't like being separated from her calf, so she kicked me."

"Oh, James. Does that happen very often? That type of accident."

"It was my own fault. My mind was elsewhere, and you can not do that in any job, not just farming. The heifer was frightened that I was going to take her calf away, so she kicked me. It is not so different to what a human would do to protect its young."

Kate shook her hair and said that that seemed dry enough. She was about to get up and sit on James' chair, when he patted the sofa beside him, and it seemed the most natural thing in the world to sit beside him. He handed Kate a glass of wine and she tucked her feet up underneath herself, laid her head against the back of the sofa, and closed her eyes momentarily. She was enjoying the feeling of comfort and closeness, which had developed between her and James, and knew that he felt the same way.

When Kate opened her eyes, James was scrutinizing her face, devouring her with his eyes. There was no mistaking his next intention. James leaned over and pressed his lips slowly and gently to hers. Kate's response was immediate and unmistakable. Any doubts that James may have had vanished at that moment. Kate seemed to enjoy his kisses as much as he enjoyed hers. With his lips still clinging to hers, he removed her wine glass, placing it on the table next to him. His strong arms went around Kate, pulling her closer into his warm, hard body. Kate thought she would drown in happiness at that moment, and was sure that James felt the same. As James went to lie back onto the sofa and pull Kate with him, there was unfortunately one thing they had forgotten.

"Oh god, I do not believe this…"

James had forgotten that he still had his cast on. He took a deep breath, attempting to calm himself, saying to Kate: "Having a cast on during lambing was bad, having it on during round up was even worse, but having a cast on when you are attempting to make love to someone … now, that's frustrating." James took a deep breath, then kissed Kate lightly on the lips, before saying, "Well, maybe it's better this way. When we finally make love, I would rather it wasn't with a plaster cast that has been in a cow shed and a lambing pen, with a lot of smelly sheep. I really, really, really would like to soak in a hot bath first.

"You do realize this is all your fault, don't you?" James said in a mock but serious tone.

"My fault? I wasn't even here."

"Exactly. It was because you weren't here that I made a school boy error – because my mind was not on my work."

James pulled Kate into the crook of his body with her back against his chest. His arms wrapped around her, holding her gently, while he started to explain how he hadn't realized that he had missed the company of a woman until she had arrived.

"I'm saying this badly, you can tell I'm out of practice. I don't just mean any woman. I mean a relationship with a woman. Jennifer and I were unhappy most of the time, after the first year of our marriage. We seemed to walk on eggshells, almost – trying not to cause an argument. Yet arguing was all we seem to do. We never talked, to be honest. Now that I look back, we had nothing in common. Oh, we were both journalists, but I had finished with that. Right or wrong, that to me was in another lifetime."

"Hey you are not going to beat yourself up over that again are you? You have paid the price for marrying Jennifer, and by now she is probably in some 'hell hole', and enjoying every damn bit of it. And you are a wonderful father to a gorgeous, happy, fabulous little cherub. So look what came out of that marriage, it wasn't all bad. You are a pretty damn good farmer, when you are not breaking your leg; and to show what a great landlord you are, why don't we have a wine and stuff your face party on Wednesday night, as a kind of celebration? We can celebrate the removal of your cast on Thursday, and Lorna and Morag's businesses, and the prodigal return of your uninvited guest – me!"

"Do you know, Kate Johnson, you are the best thing that ever landed at my gate. Uninvited, maybe, but you sure as hell are invited from now on, into my life and into our hearts. Both mine and Izzy's."

As Kate turned her face around to see his, James leaned down very slowly, and kissed Kate's soft lips with long, lingering sips, his breath coming in short gasps, as his hands roamed over her slim but curvetous figure. He stopped and put his chin on top of Kate's head, saying he thought it was time for bed, as it was difficult enough having a shower as it was – had she any idea how difficult it was putting a bin bag over the top of a plaster cast and standing upright at the same time?

"Well, it's not easy, I can tell you. And if I have to have another one, cold at that, that would also be your fault."

Chapter 20

The next few days were a blur of activity for Kate, riding around on the quad bike in the field checking ewes and lambs, making sure the mothers were taking care of their young, clearing out the lambing pens, and putting things back to the way they were until next year's lambing, as best Kate could presume. James seemed to be a cross, between excited, to get his plaster off, and even more frustrated at it still being on.

When Kate told Izzy about having a little drinks party, and asking Lorna, Keith, Morag and Eaden, Izzy was visibly excited, and asked, why?

Kate said, "Well, it's for lots of reasons. It's for your dad's horrible plaster cast coming off, and for Lorna and Morag's businesses, and to thank everyone for being so kind while I was away, while you and your dad needed lots of help on the farm.

Izzy thought for a moment, then said, "Oh, so it's a grown up party. Oh, don't worry.

I'll go to bed and be asleep really fast, so you won't have to worry about me."

Kate knelt down to Izzy's height and put her hands around her lovely little cheeks saying, "You will not go to bed, young lady. You are my right hand 'man'. Who single handedly did all the lambing? Well, apart from the help from Eaden, Keith and your dad. Between us, we almost did the lambing ourselves. Who taught me to ride the quad? Who has a thriving business and is part of the business trio? And besides, it is your home. So that makes you the host. And I rather hoped you would help me with the preparation, and I also forgot to say, it's a kind of welcome back party for me. You welcomed me back, didn't you?"

"Oh yes, Kate. I hope you never have to go away again. Dad and I missed you so much. He was really miserable without you here. Oops, I'm not supposed to say that."

"And I missed you both, more than I could ever tell. So that's our little secret."

When Kate rang Lorna and Morag to ask them if they would like to come to the house for drinks, Kate said she realized that they would be tired, as it was farmer's market on a Wednesday. They had both said in unison, you must be kidding there is nothing better for a pick-me-up than a drink and food, and that they had not prepared themselves. That's if there was food, they added almost sheepishly. Kate said not to worry, there would be plenty to eat and drink, so all they had to do was to come. They could even put their feet up if they were tired.

Lorna said she would let Kate into a little secret: that farmer's market day was like a holiday away from the farm, they loved it. They did half the work they would if they were on the farm. They chatted to all their friends who they didn't normally have time to see, and they promised every time that they will ring, but never even have time to do that. They love every minute of it, but they said, do not tell the boys, as that's our secret. Kate laughed to herself. She seemed to be collecting secrets, which made her feel really at home.

Kate and Izzy prepared enough food to feed an army, commented James. They put it in the large pantry to keep fresh for the next day. James checked, at Kate's insistence, that they had enough to drink, before Kate and Izzy drew a sigh of relief. Kate smiled at Izzy's expression of exaggerated exhaustion, and for a moment she could see what she was going to look like when she was older.

Wednesday evening came all too quickly and Kate realized she was excited. It was as though she were dressing for a date. She looked through the wardrobe of clothes, which she had thrown in her case on that terrible morning after Dominic … No, she thought, this was no time for thoughts like that, this was a social evening with her new found friends … and James. Kate got a bubbling feeling in her stomach when she thought of James and how he would look at her when she was dressed. She knew that he definitely noticed what she wore, as she saw him looking on occasions. Just as he must have noticed her watching him when she thought he was not looking.

Izzy knocked on Kate's bedroom door and asked if she could come in. Kate took Izzy's hand and said, "If my door is open, Izzy, you are welcome any time. You don't have to knock.

You're just in time to help me choose what to wear."

Kate told Izzy to jump up on the bed and she would give her a fashion show, though she didn't have that much to choose from. Kate held a 'little black number' up in front of her, and put the hanger over her neck, giving the impression that she was wearing the dress. She then gave the pose of a fashion model, who also introduced the item: "Miss Kate Johnson is modeling a sexy little black number, which every woman of today should have…"

The next ones were delivered in the same way, and Izzy was rolling around on the bed, laughing at Kate's performance. Kate's last choice was a deep purple jersey dress with a deep V-neckline that went in at the waist and just rested on the knee. "That's the one," Izzy cried, "It's lovely the colour suits you. Oh, you will look lovely in that one, Kate."

"Then the purple one it will be. I'm off for my shower, so you better skedaddle and get dressed yourself. Don't forget, you are the hostess."

Having checked all the stock, James went upstairs to change. Passing Izzy on the stairs, he gave a loud wolf whistle, saying how beautiful she looked tonight. Izzy said, "Thank you, but just you wait until you see Kate's dress. She looks gorgeous!" With the emphasis on the 'gorgeous'.

James could hardly wait. If Kate looked that good he better smarten himself up. Instead of the usual, casual working clothes, which was his usual mode of dress, he showered and changed into a Joseph Turner shirt, coloured deep lemon and complimented by a woven silk tie, navy, with lemon and blue elephants on, by the same maker. Unfortunately, because he still had his cast on, he had no choice but to wear a pair of navy cargo pants. But, though they were undoubtedly casual, they still made James look 'gorgeous', as Izzy said to him when he came downstairs.

A thought occurred to James that Izzy was trying her hand at a little match making between him and Kate. Kate took one final look in the mirror and was pleased with what she saw. It seemed a long time since she had dressed up for an occasion, and James had never really seen her in her 'posh frock', she thought. Her dress fitted over the soft curves of her shoulders and breasts, showing her trim figure to its best advantage. The V-neck showed just enough cleavage to make it interesting. Kate had brushed her thick black hair until its curls had shone, and this time her face was not disguised with makeup in order to cover any bruises.

As Kate walked down the stairs, James looked up from putting some logs on the fire - it was spring but it was still chilly in the evenings.

"Wow!" James said. "Where have you been hiding all … that?" he said, gesturing vaguely with his hands toward her shapely figure and long legs. Kate blushed to the roots of her hair. She had gotten the desired affect, but became noticeably shy at James' smoldering look.

Luckily, Izzy came in at that moment and said, "Told you so," to James.

James responded, "And you were not wrong, Izzy my girl."

James took a mocking deep breath and said, "Which of you young ladies would like a drink?"

To which Izzy laughed at her father, and the easy relaxed atmosphere was restored. That was not to say that James and Kate would not take sneaky looks at each other all night, and Izzy was not unaware of this and was euphorically happy.

Lorna and Keith arrived first, and it was lovely to see everyone not all bundled up and dressed for the arctic. Shortly after, Morag and Eaden arrived. They all said how well they had all scrubbed up, pointing out that you almost forget that you're human during lambing, and the smell seemed to linger for days.

"Right, that's enough talk about smelly sheep and cows," Morag said firmly. "At least until the women have left and the men have sneaked off to the internet."

James gave each of them a drink, which included a very strange looking drink for Izzy, complete with little umbrella. Then James took his place behind Kate and casually placed his arm around the curve of her waist. He announced that, "There would be no sneaking off, until later at least. This is a thank you night from Kate, Izzy and I, for all the help each of you gave us during lambing. We know we could not have done it without you. And I would like to thank Kate, for all her help and enthusiasm, which was a bit scary at times I must admit, but never so generously meant. I would also like to thank Izzy for all her help, though colluding with Kate into letting her ride the quad was a little devious, and I am surprised at you Izzy." James held his glass firstly to his guests. Then he turned to Kate and Izzy, and while toasting his thanks to everyone, looked directly into Kate's eyes.

Lorna nudged Keith and Morag poked Eaden in the ribs, indicating with their eyes the looks that were passing between James and Kate. Also, they all glanced at Izzy, who was taking it all in. Who says a seven year old was too young to understand what was going on. James and Kate were totally unaware that everyone in the room was watching their every move.

The night was warm and friendly, and for once the party did not split into two groups immediately. They lazed around the living room talking farming, but also business. It was obvious to Kate that Keith and Eaden saw their wives in a totally different light. It was also obvious that to help their farms survive most farmers would have to diversify. They were proud of what their wives had achieved. Not only proud, but it had brought them closer together, knowing that each couple was fighting the financial burden together.

Lorna and Morag made coughing noises to gain a bit of hush, then they both stood up, giving what they were about to say the gravity it deserved: "Lorna and I would like to thank Kate for all of her help. Not only financial, but in her total support and advice,"
Morag said, smiling at Kate. "We know that she has had more than enough problems of her own, which makes it all the more reason that we give her a special thank you. We know that without her help we could never have started the businesses and be in the position we are in today: exhausted but financially better off."

Then Lorna and Morag lifted their glasses, and Keith and Eaden said, "Here, here, to that," in total agreement.

"To Kate," everyone said in unison, and James and Izzy joined in.

Kate swallowed hard and readied to say that it was nothing, then, she changed her mind mid-sentence and said, "If it hadn't been for each and every one of you, I would never have survived the problems I have had. So the thanks are to you all."

Kate looked around the room at her friends, her good friends. The food was a great success. Izzy was the perfect hostess, until about ten, and then she said to Kate, in a whisper, "Do you think it would be all right for me to go to bed now, Kate? I think everyone has had everything they need, and I'm a little pooped."

"You my little cherub have been the perfect hostess, and deserve the rest of the evening off, so I'm ordering you to go to sleep. And thank you." Kate went down to Izzy's level and kissed her on her cheek, saying goodnight. Izzy pulled Kate a little closer so that she could whisper in her ear, saying, "Didn't I tell you that that was the dress? Dad thinks you are gorgeous. I can tell because he keeps looking at you."

Kate looked over at James, and as Izzy said that, James seemed to instinctively know that they were talking about him, and he smiled at them with a puzzled expression on his face, though his eyes once again could not help themselves from drinking in the very pleasing sight of Kate, in a way he had not seen her before.

By eleven-thirty their guests began to make noise of getting up early and wonderful evening, but they better go. Kate gave Lorna and Morag a hug, saying thank you to them both for coming and it had been the best night ever. Lorna and Morag looked at each other and decided there was no reason why they could not divulge their secret, which they had both been sworn to keep by their husbands. Lorna said, "It must be obvious to you now, anyway, Kate, that James is, erm … you know, besotted about you. It's not as though we are breaking any confidences now, because it's plain to see, when he can't keep his eyes off you."

"But when you went away," jumped in Morag, dramatically, "he was a broken man. But we were sworn by the boys not to tell you anything in the emails, because James said he didn't want you to come back from your city life for him. And that farming was something you had to be born to, and that you would eventually want to leave, just as Jennifer had. We were desperate to tell you Kate, but it would have broken his heart if you had come back for the wrong reasons; you know, because you felt sorry for him, because of his leg and all. But we have no need to worry now, because it's obvious to the world that you are as besotted as he is.

Kate also noticed that the guys were in a guilty looking huddle at the door, and then, suddenly, they were all business-like, telling Lorna and Morag to stop gossiping.

After waving the couples off, James closed the door and started to help clear the food plates and load the dishwasher. Kate almost knew that within minutes James was going to come out with something strange. She didn't know what, but she just felt that what ever it was the guys had been conspiring about involved James.

"Erm, Keith has offered to drive me into Aberdeen tomorrow to have this wretched cast off. It makes more sense than you struggling through the traffic in a city you have never been to, especially when you haven't driven for such a long time."

Whew, thought Kate, is that it or is there more? She suspected there was more, so simply replied, "Yes, I suppose you're right. It does make sense. Was Keith going into Aberdeen for something special?"

"Erm … Yes, a part for his tractor. So it's not out of the way for him. And, oh, erm, another funny thing. Would you believe it, Eaden has to drive to Edinburgh station on Friday morning to take some pottery stuff for Morag. And, you know, it crossed my mind that Izzy hasn't seen her grandparents since before Christmas, and this would be a perfect opportunity for her. What do you think? We could pick her up on Sunday, and it would give you a chance to meet my parents."

Ah, thought Kate, she could guess now what was happening: the conspiratorial looks at the back door was a little male matchmaking.

"Well, that's sounds perfect. But that means Izzy would have to take a day off school, would that be okay?"

"Oh, I'm sure. Just this once won't make that much difference at her age, and she would love to see her grandma and grandpa."

Kate could see James almost jump up and down with excitement. Her own stomach was doing summersaults as well, but she managed to control it.

As they finished clearing away, James took Kate slowly by the hand into the living room, and stopped in front of the large inglenook fireplace. He put his hands on either side of her face, saying, "Will you promise me something Kate?" Kate nodded, looking into James' eyes, which at that moment looked almost black.

"Will you wear that dress again when I get this horrible cast off, and I'm able to take full advantage of you?"

Kate laughed at James' candor, and promised she would wear it anytime he wished, and that he could definitely take advantage of her.

"Izzy said you would like this dress."

"Like it? You look 'gorgeous', as Izzy would say. It's enough to drive a man with a cast on mad."

Chapter 21

James was up extra early to do his chores before changing to go to Aberdeen with Keith. The excitement in the house was palpable from each and every one of them. Izzy had been told that tomorrow she would be having the day off school and going to see her grandparents – what child would not be excited at that prospect?

James was excited because he was going to be free of the terrible incumbent, which had dogged him since Kate had come back, and also the prospect of two whole nights of being a bachelor once again. His *decree nisi* had meant nothing to James when it arrived in the post one day without warning. He had no intentions of seeing anyone for a very long time; therefore, it would make very little difference to him if he were single or married. This was the first time he had actually given a relationship a thought, and his stomach felt butterflies of excitement. James told himself to calm down, for God's sake. He was behaving like a love struck teenager instead of a man in his middle and respectable years.

Outwardly Kate seemed to be going about her normal morning without a disturbing thought in her head. In actual fact, she had no idea what she was doing. At one point she found herself lifting the lid of the Aga and about to put the milk jug onto it instead of into the fridge. She stopped herself, just in time, from making a fool of herself, and having to explain what she was thinking about.

Kate wasn't sure how she was going to get through the day. All her thoughts would be about the two whole nights that James and she would be in the house alone. All by themselves, with no one else here, though Kate again, letting her mind drift off until Izzy's voice said, "School bus time, Kate."

"Oh, sorry Izzy. I was miles away. Elsa and I will walk with you, as it's such a lovely morning."

The mini school bus picked its occupants up at the track road ends. The driver knew every child at every pick up point and every child knew all of the drivers. Even though the weather could be treacherous, it was very rare that the bus didn't arrive. Most of the drivers were semi-retired, so they were fairly elderly, yet they were a rare breed of driver. Kate wondered what kind of weather it would have to be to stop the bus from carrying out its journey. Izzy was sure their motto was 'the school must go on', because even when she hoped the school would be frozen or flooded, or blown away, the bus still arrived.

It was a beautiful morning. The warm sun shone down promising a lovely day. Spring was edging its way toward summer and the cuckoo was calling for a mate. Izzy had explained to Kate that the cuckoo call was lovely when it first arrived, at the back end of April, but after a while you wished it would hurry up and find a mate, because the constant chirping gets on your nerves.

Kate waved to Izzy as the bus pulled away. She stood there in a little world of her own, the sun warm on her face, the swallows dive bombing as they swished passed her toward the open barn door where they would make a nest and lay eggs. Kate stopped and said to Elsa, "Good grief, does everything breed up here in Scotland, or have the nesting instinct? It must be catching."

James was standing beside Keith's old jeep, obviously waiting for Kate before leaving for Aberdeen. He said he hoped to be back for tea time but he had no idea how long these things took. He smiled the smile that lingered as if there were more he wanted to say. Kate thought, if Keith had not been watching, she felt sure James would have kissed her goodbye, but their relationship was still in its embryonic stage and not ready for open scrutiny. She waved them both off and watched them drive away up the track towards the gate before turning to go into the house. Kate said to Elsa, who by now was settling back down in her bed, "Well that's what you're doing today, but what am I going to do?" Kate realized this was the very first time she had actually been left on her own at the farm.

After clearing the kitchen table and loading the dish washer, Kate decided that she would change the beds, as the sun was shining and there was a soft breeze. It made her want to wash things.

Good grief, she thought. Is that another sign that I am nesting, wanting everything shipshape. No, she reasoned with herself, poor

James had slept in his bed with that horrible cast on his leg, wouldn't it be lovely for him if he could sleep in a lovely clean bed.

Kate walked into James' room feeling as though she were trespassing. She felt as though she had deliberately waited until he wasn't there to snoop. But surely snoop was too strong a word, thought Kate; however, she had had a fascination to look around James' room ever since the day she left the note for him, and she hadn't time to do other than smell the fragrance, which seemed to wrap itself around James.

Kate fulfilled the pretence of stripping off the sheets, duvet cover and pillow cases, until her eyes could not help straying around the room. On the tall boy chest of drawers, which were very old pine, there was a very old, brass, ornate picture frame. In the picture were three people, one of which was clearly James. They were all dressed in evening dress. The elderly couple were quite obviously James' parents. On one side of the three was a really elegant man, roughly the same height as James, with silver grey hair and a pencil thin mustache. On the opposite side was James, looking absolutely gorgeous in evening dress. And between the two of them was a slightly smaller woman dressed in a beautiful, long evening dress, with a stole of the same material around her shoulders. Each of the smiling gentlemen had a hand on one of the woman's shoulders, seemingly drawing her closer. Whatever the event, it was obviously a grand affair, and they looked every bit at home.

On the opposite side of the dresser was a picture of James proudly holding, who Kate knew to be, Izzy as a toddler. It was clear to see that both father and child idolized each other. Both of them obviously found something very funny, and the picture was snapped just at that moment, capturing the happy memory for ever.

Kate could not help herself. She wandered around the room, picking things up then replacing them, trying to make sense of the man she knew as a farmer, yet knowing he was also a journalist, therefore educated. But there was even more to James. Kate idly opened the wardrobe and glanced at James' clothes. She fingered what were, quite obviously, handmade suits, sport jackets, and cavalry twill trousers in various shades. There were shelves of dress and casual shirts, all neatly organized. James obviously had a very good dress sense; however, he also had a quirky side to his clothes: his ties were all woven silk, even the bow ties, but in the most extraordinary colours and styles – stripes, dots, flowers, and the elephant one he wore the other evening. An old china trinket tray inside the wardrobe on the shelf was full of another of James' quirky choices: cufflinks. Cufflinks of all shapes and sizes, from evening wear to nautical knots.

It had become obvious to Kate, as she had fingered through James' clothes, that they were the trappings of a gentleman. Oh, he was a farmer and a journalist, but he was also a gentleman. Somehow that did not surprise her. James' whole demeanor said as much. Yet he had seen such poverty that he could blend and mix with people from any walk of life. This endeared James, more than ever, to Kate. He must have despised his privileged life, causing him terrible feelings of guilt when he saw situations that he could not change for those involved, how ever sorry he felt for them.

Kate felt as though she had seen a side to James which was only known to those closest to him.

She closed his wardrobe doors feeling that she had somehow intruded into this private life. Not just snooping through his clothes to satisfy a woman's curiosity, but actually prying into his private life. With a deep sigh, she vowed that, if and when she got to know James better, she would admit to this transgression and hope he understood.

The day passed much faster than Kate thought possible. In fact, she had only just replaced all the clean bedding on both Izzy and James' beds, vacuumed their rooms, and had a light lunch, when James rang to say he and Keith were on their way back, and that it should take less than an hour. Kate got the feeling that James again would have said more, but it would appear he was on his mobile phone. Normally, at Comraich, there is no signal, so nobody bothers switching on their mobiles, even if they have one. In the city, it's the first thing everyone did when they woke up: check to see if anyone had texted them during the night. It was amazing to think that Kate, who was just as bad when she lived in the city, had not even turned hers on since she left Manchester.

Kate could hear Izzy coming down the track singing her little heart out about 'no more school, no more school, no more school, tomorrow'. Kate smiled; she remembered singing that song when school broke up for a holiday. Izzy was obviously very excited about having the day off tomorrow, allowing her an early start to her holiday weekend with her grandparents. It crossed Kate's mind that if excitement were measured in watts, there would be enough energy to light up the house without the generator, if you took into consideration hers' and James's excitement, too.

Keith dropped James off at the gate at the end of the track. James obviously wanted to walk to the farm unaided and without his cast. The hospital had given him a walking stick to use for a while until he got the flexibility back in the knee; however, James was determined that he was not going to be an invalid, and would manage perfectly well without it.

James walked into the kitchen proudly, without his cast. Kate and Izzy cheered and whistled as James rolled his torn trouser leg above the knee, as if to prove that there was no cast. Kate said, in an imitation circus voice, "And for his next trick, Mister James Wallace will walk unaided across the kitchen floor." To which James walked across the floor, playing the game, and Izzy and Kate cheered again.

Kate had just had time before James and Izzy got home to make a sandwich cake, something she hadn't done for a very long time. She had also quickly butter iced it, and stuck a candle she found from one of Izzy's previous birthdays in the middle. They announced that James must blow out the candle to bring luck in not breaking his other leg.

James said thank you to both, putting his arm across his body and bowing as though to an audience. They were all very happy, all three of them. It was as though each one sensed that life couldn't get any better than it was at this moment.

"How on earth did you make a cake using the Aga?"

"Well, it may look good, but I won't take any praise until you have tasted it. It may be hard as a rock bun or totally uncooked in the middle. But I will make friends with that oven if it's the last thing I do."

The whole evening went in a similar vein: happy and excited. Izzy asked Kate what she thought she should pack in her little suitcase for her holiday, and between Kate and Izzy they went through most of Izzy's clothes, saying too small, too warm, not smart enough, as Izzy tended to wear all her clothes for the farm. It became very clear why Grandma had bought Izzy the new dress and tights for Christmas, as Izzy was indeed in need of a woman's touch when it came to her wardrobe.

"Izzy, when you come back, you and I are going to go to Aberdeen and buy you some new clothes. I know you like to wear clothes which are suitable for the farm, but you also need some dress clothes."

Expecting an argument from Izzy, Kate was surprised when Izzy said, "Oh can we? I would love that Kate. Daddy will give you money to buy anything," Izzy said, with the innocence of a child. "He is always asking me if I need anything, but I don't really know, as I never go shopping except when I go with Grandma and Grandpa."

"No problem, young lady. Shopping is my forte," Kate said with a flourish, telling Izzy that she would have to hold her down, as she could buy clothes until the cows come home, so to speak.

Kate stood on the landing between Izzy's room and her own, watching James for a moment or two before eventually asking what he was doing. He must have walked up and down the stairs at least ten times, and at first Kate thought he had forgotten something and went back down to collect it.

"I am exercising. The more I exercise, the faster I can be without the cane. I just need to get the muscle tone back into the calf and the flexibility back in the knee, and I will be back to normal."

"James, I don't think the hospital meant to do it all in one day, it will come back. What's the hurry? Lambing is over, and we are managing quite well between us all, aren't we?"

"That is exactly it, you should not have to be doing manual work. You are a … guest," said James.

Actually, Kate wasn't really happy about that description of her position here. Yet she knew it to be true. What more did she expect?

James was running a bath in the family bathroom, as his en suite was a shower. As he filled the bath Kate could smell all kinds of delicious smells coming out of the bathroom. She called to Izzy within earshot of James, saying, "Who says women do all the pampering – look at the bubbles in that bath and the smell. What is that? It's too good to be a man's splash-on, surely?"

"Oh, that's Dad's posh smellies. It's gorgeous, isn't it? I think it's Calvin Klein."

"Do you not think I deserve to soak in that bath all night, with every conceivable smelly item in the water? Have I not smelled like a cross between a sheep and a cow for six weeks?" James asked.

"Well, we were too well mannered to say anything to you, but as you said it yourself…" said Kate and Izzy, laughing at James' hurt expression, saying they were only joking, and it hadn't been too bad, really, teasing him all the more.

James disappeared into the bathroom, and he was obviously not kidding about staying in all night. By the time he emerged, Izzy was ready for bed. She was all packed, and was reminding her father that she must not sleep in, as Eaden would be coming in the morning at eight thirty.

"As if you would ever sleep in, Izzy! Don't worry. You will not be late. We will be ready for Eaden."

James walked into Izzy's bedroom and took her hand, saying he was going to miss her, and asking if she knew that she was his favorite Isabella in the whole world. Izzy said as she always did when he said that to her: That she was probably the only Isabella he knew in the whole world. James hugged Izzy close, and Izzy said to James in his ear, in a whisper that made his ear tickle, "Will you be nice to Kate when I'm not here? Because she really, really, likes you, you know?"

James looked at Izzy's innocent little face, and with a puzzled expression, he said, quite seriously, for her not to worry, that he was going to be extra nice to Kate, he promised. When Kate went in to say goodnight to Izzy, leaning over to kiss her cheek, Izzy did the same as she had to James, and said to Kate: would Kate be nice to her dad while she was away, because he really, really likes you, Kate pulled back and looked into Izzy's face and wondered if, instead of a cherub, she was playing cupid.

Chapter 22

Friday morning dawned very, very, early. Even for James, as Izzy must have been up at five o'clock at least. She had written last minute instructions as to how many times Dad had to check the incubator as she had eggs in, which were due to hatch in about five days, and the note reminded him that he better check, because you can never be totally sure – one or two might hatch before. James also had to collect the eggs from the hens, keeping them separate, because she was going to sell them for breeding: pure breeds. Kate's eyes rose as she glanced at James who was taking his instructions from his seven year old daughter very seriously. Yes, he said twice over, he understood and he would not forget, and was she ready, because Eden would be pulling up any minute?

When Eaden arrived, Izzy gave James and Kate a massive hug, then got into the jeep, shouting through the open window, miss you, love you, as they drove down the track to the gate.

"Wow, was that a whirl wind or what?" Kate said, smiling and blowing out a deep breath.

"She is such a bundle of energy and a presence about the farm that, when it was suggested by the school that she would probably benefit from a boarding school education, the idea horrified me. I may be selfish, but she keeps me going, and I could not bear to send her away."

"Oh no, how terrible during the best years of a child's life. And what could she learn at boarding school that she can not learn here on the farm and at the local school, there is more to life than education alone."

"Do you know, you surprise me a little, saying that. I thought you would have been a strict educationalist, as you attended night school and extra classes to gain your knowledge."

"Well don't forget I was not happy at home, and I was not given the opportunity to be educated that Izzy will be given, when the time comes. Izzy is very fortunate. She has you, and the farm, and wonderful friends who also care for her. And though I have not met your parents I am sure they would give her total support if and when the time ever came. No, if I ever have any children of my own," Kate said, with the merest hint of a shadow crossing her face, "I would enjoy every minute of their childhood, soak it all up. I would spend time being silly with them – be a friend as well as a parent."

"It shows. I can see exactly how you would be. You're so good with Izzy, and she has never been so happy having another woman and a friend in the house. Speaking of Izzy, we should have a look at Muffin and the eggs. Then I wondered if you would like to have a little hack on Sapphire?"

"Hack?" said Kate with a puzzled expression, "Would I be showing my city upbringings if I said I didn't know what you meant by that?"

James explained that, as Kate had never been on a horse before, literally just sitting on a horse and letting the horse do the walking was hacking. Kate was really excited, and said she would love to, but she wasn't sure if she would be any good, but she was more than willing to have a go.

They went down to the barn and for James it was a great relief not to have to limp down with his crutches. Muffin was as Izzy had left her.

"No chicks have hatched," said James, "So all is well and I have done as I was told. That's what dads are for, you know."

James opened Sapphire's stall, talking softly to her, saying Kate had come to take her out. Kate walked slowly in, so as not to scare her, and as James started to collect the saddle and the tack, Sapphire knew that she was going out and was visibly excited.

"Don't worry, she won't jump about. It's just that I have not been able to exercise the horses with my leg being broken, so they are really keen to get out. But she is gentle."

James saddled Sapphire for Kate and then went to saddle Glen. Kate, however, didn't go into Glen's stall. She was a little afraid of him. As James brought Glen out of the stall he tethered him temporarily while he got a mounting block for Kate. This may not seem dignified, but until you can mount on your own, it's easier. Kate walked onto the mounting block then put her left foot in the stirrup. James held onto Sapphire's bridle with one hand, helping Kate to mount with the other. He had insisted that she wear a hard hat and fasten the chin strap, just as he did when Izzy rode.

Once mounted, Kate said it seemed awfully high from where she was sitting, but she still felt confident that Sapphire knew that she was a novice, and that Sapphire would not run away with her.

James led Sapphire out and Kate thought he would use the mounting block for himself, seeing as how his leg had only just come out of plaster, but James just seemed to jump and he was in the saddle. They walked slowly out of the barn and Kate was surprised at how much of the horse's movements she could feel through the saddle. Before long they were walking along the track. When Sapphire walked Kate seemed to sway from side to side, and it was almost a rocking motion which felt perfectly natural.

James and Kate walked side by side, and Kate's face was a picture of concentration and enjoyment. James said, "Hey you don't need to worry. Just relax, Sapphire won't run off with you. There is nothing else to it, you have done the hard bit, now sit back and relax. I thought you might like to see Comraich House…"

"Oh, I would love to see the house, James. I have seen it from a distance and it looks fascinating."

Kate took a deep breath, drinking in the beautiful day. Riding on a horse and being with James, could it get any better than this?

As they approached the house, James looked at Kate, taking in her expression as she gazed at the grandeur of it. She said she could see that it was a large house from a distance, but nothing had prepared her for how grand it was. It had massive shutters at the floor to ceiling windows, that's why she thought, when she looked from a distance, the windows had looked like eye sockets without the eyes. Now that she was close up she could see how beautiful it would be with all the shutters open. It was like a doll's house on which the massive door was in the centre of the house, just as though someone had built the house like a child's painting.

"Oh, James. How wonderful! But it looks sad, because there is no one living in it and the shutters are closed. It needs sun and light and laughter. Oh – I'm off fantasizing again."

James took both of his feet out of the stirrups and slid off of Glen's back. He came over to Kate and told her how to dismount, and then he put his hands around her waist and helped her to the ground. As she dismounted Sapphire her body slid down James' body, until they were standing together, their bodies still touching, his hands still holding her waist.

James asked, in a breathless voice, if Kate would like to have a look around the house. James obviously didn't realize that wild horses wouldn't have stopped Kate having a snoop.

James tethered the horses to a tree. Then they walked up to the house, which unbelievably was not locked. Kate could not get over the fact that the front door was unlocked. James found this amusing asking who she thought was going to come past the farm and drive up the track, where they could be seen, and then break into an empty house. Kate was too habitually entrenched in city life, where every apartment door had a lock and chain on it for security.

As they walked into the main entrance hall light filtered through the open door causing a shaft of light to illuminate the huge oak staircase and very high ceiling. As they walked into the lobby, which was as big as most people's lounge, there were very large double doors to the left and right, which Kate presumed were the main reception rooms. As each side of the front of the house had a floor to ceiling window, James opened the double doors to the left, and they walked into the most elegant room, other than a function room at a restaurant, Kate had ever seen. A large marble fireplace dominated the chimney breast and on either side were two arched alcoves. The room had a very high ceiling with a beautiful ceiling rose and matching coving around the room. It had a massive window, and when James went over to open the shutters the room suddenly flooded with sunlight.

"Oh James, how absolutely gorgeous, as Izzy would say! But there is no other word for it. It's criminal that the house is not lived in, or is it? Is this where your parents stay when they come?"

"No, no. Mother and father stopped living in either property once I got married to Jennifer. Jennifer and I lived here for the short time she was here. When my parents come to stay it's usually Christmas. They stay in the farm only two weeks of the year, and I think they are even finding even that rather difficult with Dad's poor health."

After viewing the whole of downstairs they walked up the deep, wide staircase and James opened one of the large doors. "This was one of the first rooms mother and father renovated. It was their bedroom." James walked over to the window and opened the shutters letting the light flood the room. The main wall had the most beautiful wallpaper on from the dado rail upwards, and the paper had a Chinese theme with bamboo stalks on, and Chinese birds of every colour imaginable. There was a King-size bed against one wall, yet it looked dwarfed by the sheer size of the room.

"Oh, James! Can you imagine waking up in that bed and seeing the view out of the window every day when you woke up?"

Kate gazed out of the window at the view, which stretched out in front of her as far as the eye could see. James came up behind her and put his arms around her, saying that he and Jennifer had the same view from their bedroom, which was next door, yet they had not had any pleasure from it.

James used his arms to bring Kate even closer to him, "Nothing is wonderful or special if you are not happy. We were never happy from the day we came back." James said he wondered if he would ever be happy again in this house, which his parents had so lovingly restored, and it had brought his parents even closer.

Kate turned around so that she faced James, his arms still wrapped around her. "You don't mean that, James. This house is a happy house. I can feel it." She lifted her hand to his face, saying it just wants to be loved again, it needs a family.

Slowly but purposefully James brought his lips down onto Kate's. Within seconds it was as though someone had lit the touch paper. They were passionately entwined: stroking, kissing, and running their hands over each other's bodies as though they needed to remember where everything was. James started to walk backwards toward the large bed and as his legs touched the mattress he lifted Kate onto it, and within seconds they were lying together: kissing, touching, and groaning as the excitement spiralled out of control. At that moment James pulled back and looked at Kate. Are you sure Kate? This is what you want?"

James thought, no matter how much he desperately wanted to make love to Kate, he wanted to be sure it was what they both wanted. Her answer was yes …yes … yes, as she pulled James' head down to hers once again, so that their lips and bodies fused together.

****

It had been obvious to everyone since Christmas. The electricity between Kate and James could have lit up a room. Their pent up frustration of the last week was so noticeable that Keith and Eaden had conspired to make sure James and Kate had this weekend together undisturbed. They could not trust James to engineer a situation as he was too much of a gentleman and they knew he would not take advantage of Kate under his own roof with Izzy at home. The tenants of Comraich farms were conspicuous by their absence that weekend, and that included the wives, who were for once in total agreement with their husbands.

As Kate and James lay in the middle of the large bed, still wrapped in each others arms, a pool of sunlight streamed through the long window and warmed their naked bodies. James' arms wrapped around Kate as though he thought she might escape if he let go. Their clothes lay where they were thrown in their haste to become one.

James said, with a voice so satiated that he could hardly form his words, "Marry me Kate Johnson. Be my wife, my lover, and my friend." James held his breath waiting for Kate's answer, hoping he had not been too hasty. He could not stop himself. The words were out before he could stop them.

Kate's heart skipped a beat, and she replied, "Does Izzy come with that proposal?"

. "She does." said James, hoping he was right about Kate.

"Then I accept your proposal, James Wallace."

"I knew you loved Izzy as much as you love me. You do love me, don't you Kate?"

Kate looked up at James' face with passion beaming from her dark eyes. It was unmistakable that she loved him profoundly. They kissed and caressed each other, making love again until the shadows were streaming through the long windows. Kate delighted in the musky smell of his familiar cologne, now mixed with perspiration and their love making. James drank in the perfume on Kate's skin, which seemed to intensify with the exertion of their love.

The light was fading fast when Kate and James eventually began to get dressed remembering the horses were tethered outside. "They will be fine," James told Kate. "They will have munched on the grass and won't have even noticed how long we have been away. Come over here, Kate Johnson."

Kate went over to where James was standing, in front of the window watching the sun sink behind the horizon. He said, "If you will share mine and Izzy's life then I think we should give Comraich another try. What do you think?"

"Oh James, I will always love this house. This room, especially, will always hold a special place in my heart. And what happened to you and Jennifer was not the fault of the house, nor the curse of Comraich. It was a mistake. You were both searching for something, but unfortunately not the same thing. That was not the fault of the house. Your parents were very happy here, and we will be happy too. I promise."

They rode back to the house slowly, enjoying each other's company and every last moment of the day. The last of the birds chirped in the distance before settling into the darkness. James looked over to Kate and she looked him full in the face with unashamed satiated love. It was probably a good job they did not meet anyone on the track, as James looked so smug and satisfied, like a large Cheshire cat. The act of having his hands around Kate's waist, while simply lifting her back onto Sapphire's back, was enough to start James pulse rising again. The sooner they got back to the farm the better, for both of them.

Chapter 23

James and Kate spent half of the night in James' bed talking in hushed voices, as though their love making was a secret they were not ready to reveal to anyone. They talked of hopes and fears, things they wished they had done differently, things they would still like to do. One of James' wishes was to write again, but under his own name and not for any psychological or cathartic reason, simply because he had always enjoyed writing. He never seemed to have the time anymore, or was that his excuse? They spoke frankly, and Kate made an observation, saying to James that maybe he filled his time so successfully that he genuinely didn't have time to write, though it was not by design. James agreed that Kate was probably right and he promised he would do something about it.

They discussed living in Comraich house itself, and about the farm. James said he would still like to have some input, but that he would put a farm manager in again. They talked about how Izzy would take to Kate being her new mother, and when they would break the news to her. As soon as we collect her from my parents, said James, and will announce our engagement at the same time? James said, with a questioning look, to Kate. Kate agreed, though she was nervous about announcing their engagement to James' parents, because she did not know them, they would not know anything about her, and she would come as a shock to them. She knew that Izzy would love it, of that she was sure.

They talked long into the night until once again they made slow, but satisfying love, before eventually going to sleep in each others arms.

James could not remember a morning, while living on the farm, when he didn't want to get out of bed. Kate had rolled over and he had quite naturally rolled over with her and curved his arm around her waist. As soon as he moved to get up, Kate turned to face him saying, "Hi. I've been awake for ages, but I didn't want to move. I was enjoying having your arm around me."

"Good morning. Well, one good reason for getting in a farm manager would be that I could share the chores with him, and when I want to spend time with my wife I will let him do the early morning jobs. You stay in bed get some more rest. I must go and feed the stock."

"I will not let you get up all on your own. I will get up and make breakfast for you. You have used a lot of energy in the night, you will need topping up," Kate said with a suggestive tone to her voice. James pulled her out of the bed, threatening to dunk her in the shower. Seeing the look in Kate's eyes, which seemed to say that it was not a bad idea, James said that she had best not tempt him, at least until tonight – his poor animals were starving and waiting for him.

The day passed swiftly and they both enjoyed every minute of each other's company. They did the ordinary things that they always did, but for some reason everything seemed to have an excitement about it: knowing that at the end of the day, instead of simply sitting, talking with a glass of wine, they would go to bed together and make love again.

Sunday came all too soon, the day that James and Kate would make their announcement to his parents. Kate was nervous about that, but James assured her that his parents would love her. Kate dressed very soberly, so as to give the impression to James' parents that she was a sensible woman and not some frivolous numpty. She wore one of the only jackets she had brought with her. It was a jacket in pure silk, in the style of a hound's tooth Jacket. It had four buttons down the front and a notched collar underneath. She wore a pure silk blouse of soft cream and a pair of cream chinos. The belt on her chinos was dark brown, matching the tan and brown check of the jacket. She wore tan pumps and carried a matching leather handbag. She added a splash of Jo Malone and a final flick to her hair, once again talking to herself, telling herself that if this didn't 'knock 'em dead', then nothing would.

Kate hadn't heard James come into her bedroom, where her clothes were in the wardrobe, until he came up behind her and she saw his face in the mirror as he put his arms around her.

"You look like a model. You look 'gorgeous', as Izzy would say. And you smell good enough to eat."

As James turned her round to kiss her, Kate stood back a little so that she could see James' outfit. "Wow, 'handsome man'! You are a dark horse aren't you? *You* are the one that looks like a model, a male model. And you smell so delicious. Do you know, I have a confession to make: when I was changing your sheets, I looked at your gorgeous clothes in the wardrobe. But to be honest, they never looked like they do now with you in them…"

James had on a navy blue blazer by Joseph Turner, and a coordinating JT Shirt with fine blue and yellow stripes, which he wore casual with no tie. He also wore cream chinos with a leather belt and navy loafers, and to finish it all off, he smelled of his usual, absolutely fabulous, Hugo Boss.

Kate said, what she wouldn't do to stay here and seduce James, instead of meeting his parents. James said again how they would love her, they would respect his choice, and that, if he knew Izzy, she will have talked their ears off about you, so stop worrying.

James had brought the Land Rover out of the garage and Kate realized that she had never been in a car with James. He opened the door for her, which was something she knew he would do. There was something about James, especially dressed the way he was. He was every inch the gentleman, just as Lorna and Morag had said, and they had not only been referring to his manners.

The drive to Edinburgh was pleasant. James was a competent driver and handled the large vehicle skilfully. Kate was very nervous, but hopeful. If James' parents were anything like him, they would be well mannered, so she would not feel uncomfortable. It was more than that though. She really wanted them to like her, as James had asked her to marry him, and they were obviously a great part of James' and Izzy's life. She wanted to part of the happy family life, which James and Izzy both shared.

"You are very quiet," said James, and put his hand across to cover hers, which was resting on her leg. "They are gong to love you, just as I do," he said, with such sincerity that Kate suddenly had the courage to believe he may be right. She did not have any more time to worry as they slowly pulled to a halt in front of, what could only be described as, a mansion.

"Didn't you say your parents had an apartment in Edinburgh?"

"Well, we call it the apartment in comparison to Comraich. It is a house, but they tend to live on the top floor since they had the stair lift put in, mainly because of the views over Edinburgh."

As they got out of the Land Rover, Kate looked up. 'Gob smacked' would be the expression she was looking for: this was not an apartment building, as she had first thought. This was James' parents' home: this four story, stone built, Georgian Town House, probably eighteenth century, but Kate could not be sure of that, she told herself, sarcastically, as she was absorbing her thoughts about the house.

As they started to mount the stone stairs towards the very large heavy front door, which had beautiful old fashioned heavy brass furniture on, the door sprung open.

"Dad! Kate! Oh, I've missed you so much. I have so much to tell you. And Grandma and Grandpa are dying to meet Kate. They are going to love you, and you will love them, Kate."

Kate and James each had a cuddle of Izzy and joined in the excitement of seeing her after only a few days. They had not realized how much joy she brought into their daily lives. Izzy noticed immediately that her Dad and Kate were close. She noticed that her father had his arm around the back of Kate, and as a result Izzy was practically jumping up and down. "I must go and tell Grandpa something. Hurry up and come upstairs." Izzy certainly did not wait to take a ride on the chair lift, unlike when she first arrived. This time she took the stairs two at a time, practically bursting to tell Grandma something before they got up stairs.

Kate and James started up the wide stair case together. James took Kate's hand in his and lifted her fingers to his lips, saying quietly, "I love you."

Kate smiled back, mouthing that she loved him too. As they got to the top of the stairs they were greeted by the elegant woman with silver hair who Kate had seen in the photograph in James' room. She was standing just outside the lounge door waiting for them to come up the stairs. She leaned close to James and kissed his cheek.

"James, darling! It's been too long. And this must be Kate – I have been so looking forward to meeting you. We have heard so much about you from Izzy. I hope you don't mind me not coming down to greet you, having Izzy to open the door is a real boon. Andrew and I are not as young as we were, and we find the stairs a bit heavy going, that's why we have had the chair lift installed. It is an amazing contraption.

"Oh, my dear, I'm so sorry. I'm becoming senile. I'm Ailsa, James' mother. Do come in and meet his father. Andrew, dear, this is Kate."

A very smart gentleman, with silver grey hair and a very dapper moustache, which made him look quite military, started to rise from his chair. Kate said immediately not to get up,

347

please, but Andrew stood to his full height, of probably six feet tall, a little short of James, saying nonsense, nonsense, I am not dead yet, just a little weak at present.

"How do you do, my dear? You are as pretty as Izzy said you were. And no mistake, I can see what James sees in you. Hello, I'm James' father. Just you call me Andy, my dear."

"Hello, I'm, err, Kate, as you know by now. I think Izzy has probably told you about me. All good things I hope, Izzy? I am so very pleased to meet you both."

"My dear, Izzy has spoken of nothing else: how you spent Christmas with them, how you were caught in the snow storm and had to stay over Christmas and New Year, and how much they missed you when you went back to Manchester, but how you came back and helped with the lambing, even doing the night shift. Oh yes, Izzy has told us all about you."

This was all said very tongue in cheek by Ailsa, with Andy trying to smother a smile. Ailsa put Kate out of her misery by saying, "One day you will tell us all about it yourself, my dear. I'm sure it is a fascinating story. Ailsa gave Kate the

348

most conspiratorial look and then winked at her outrageously while squeezing her hand kindly. Kate knew immediately she was going to love this couple just as she did their son.

Just as Kate was breathing a sigh of relief, James coughed and said, "Is it my turn now? Mother, Father, Izzy … Kate and I have something to tell you."

"I told you so, I told you so! And, oh, this is the best news ever," said Izzy excitedly.

"But I haven't told you anything yet," said James, watching all the expectant faces, knowing that they had already guessed what he was about to say. However, he wanted to do this properly, as he never had before. James took hold of Kate's hand and smiled into her eyes before saying: "Kate and I would like to announce our engagement."

Izzy was jumping up and down. Ailsa came over to hug both of them saying she could not be happier. Andy was a true gentleman. He came over and asked if he could kiss his future daughter in law. Kate gave him a kiss and said she knew that she was going to love being part of this family, as all the men were gentlemen and all the women were absolute angels, the latter said while looking at Izzy's excited little face.

"Maybe, young lady, you are actually a 'cupid'. You seem to know a lot more than we knew. Your dad and I didn't even know ourselves until this weekend that we love each other," Kate said, stumbling a little over the new words to describe James' and her relationship.

"Oh, I knew ages ago, simply ages ago that dad loved you. And I knew you loved him because you were so nice to him all the time. And I saw him kiss you when you were on the quad bike and he was so worried about you. And today, when dad was holding your hand, I knew you were going to tell Grandma and Grandpa. That's why I had to warn them."

James' father shook his sons hand firmly, saying, this is the one, James: "I told you there was a woman out there who would be right for you, didn't I?"

Ailsa hugged her son, kissing his cheek, saying she could not believe she could be so happy at her age, and that you never know. She said, in a stage whisper, "We might even have another grandchild before we pop our clogs."

Ailsa said to Izzy with a wink and a smile, would she show Kate round the house while she and grandpa had a little word with her father. Izzy knew that this always meant that grandma wanted rid of her while they discussed something private. Kate was still in a bit of a daze after all the excitement, and when Izzy took her by the hand saying come and look at the house, Kate went with her without question.

When Kate eventually began to take in what she was seeing she felt as though she should have paid an entrance fee at the door. The house was more like a museum of antiques: homely, but so grand she could not imagine anyone actually living in it. The ceilings were so high and ornate she had never seen the like, except in stately homes. The floors were polished wood with beautiful oriental rugs covering a huge portion of the room.

Kate and Izzy, walked from room to room, and Kate could hardly take in the absolute splendor. Izzy never gave it a thought. The house was simply Grandma and Grandpa's house, just as Lorna and Keith's farm was simple but homely, as was Morag and Eaden's, Comraich farm was home and Comraich house was somewhere she didn't even remember living in, it was just a house.

When the tour was finally over they walked back towards the upstairs apartment where her grandparents lived. Izzy slid her little hand into Kate's and said, looking up at Kate's face, "I am so glad Dad fell in love with you, because I loved you from the very beginning, and I told Grandpa and Grandma: Dad should marry you and you could come and live with us forever." Out of the mouths of babes, thought Kate.

When they arrived back at the sitting room, Kate and Izzy knew that something was about to be announced. There was a silver tray with four glasses on and Andy was opening a bottle of something, which looked suspiciously like champagne. James walked over to Kate and took hold of her hand, saying to her that, in his family, there was a tradition of choosing a family ring for the bride to be. But, if for any reason she did not like the ring he had chosen for her, she could wear it as a dress ring. There was absolutely no pressure for her to have it as her engagement ring.

James opened the little dark blue jewellery box, and in it was the most exquisite sapphire ring surrounded by diamonds cut in the shape of a lozenge. Kate gave a small gasp, saying how gorgeous it was, and that she really hoped it fit because she loved it.

"Then, Kate Johnson, will you do me the honour of being my wife?" James asked. He took the ring from its setting and placed it on Kate's finger only to find that it fitted perfectly and could, in actual fact, have been made for her.

"Oh yes, James Wallace, I certainly will marry you. And I will also be the mother of your adorable little cherub, Isabella."

The End

Epilogue

Kate and James were married in August. The wedding was held at Comraich house. When Kate and James broke the news to Lorna, Morag, Keith and Eaden they had all cheered, saying thank goodness for that, and hadn't he taken his time about it. Lorna and Morag insisted to Kate that they would love to decorate the house and prepare the food for the wedding. James told Kate she could have anything she wanted, which included professional services for everything if she wished; however, Kate said she would be honoured if Lorna and Morag would arrange her wedding for her, because, she said, they were the best businesses in Scotland.

The day of the wedding dawned and the weather was delightful. It was warm and breezy and the house stood proud on top of the hill, in the centre of the neatly manicured lawns. Eaden and Keith had arranged for two large gazebos to be set up on either side of the door to the house. Red velvet chairs had been arranged on either side for family and friends. Keith and Eaden had insisted on cutting the lawns and arranging everything outdoors as their wives did everything indoors. They insisted that it was their gift to their friends and neighbors.

When Andy and Ailsa came up from the farm where they were staying they took one look at the house and Ailsa said to her husband, emotion causing her to have to swallow hard, "That is the way the house should be and will be from now on Andy, the way it should always have been. A happy house, loved, just as it was when we lived there."

It was not a large wedding, only close friends and family, which was the way James and Kate wanted it to be. James watched his daughter come down the large oak staircase looking like an absolute angel, her dark curls framing her beautiful little face, which beamed with pride at being a bridesmaid. Her dress was the palest lemon silk, which complimented her dark colouring to perfection. She had matching silk pumps on and a tiny little dolly bag fastened around her wrist.

James thought he could not be more proud of his daughter until her own wedding day. Izzy came and stood with her father and watched while Kate walked down the staircase, just as she had. James was speechless, Kate looked like a goddess. Her jet black curls held only by a silver comb in the centre of her hair, her shoulders bare and her olive skin showing off the whiteness of the dress, making it appear to glow. The bodice was tight fitting, showing the curve of her breasts as it tapered down to her tiny waist. It gradually flared out slightly showing the shape of her hips.

Her flowers were not large or ornate. They were a simple posy of wild flowers. James came forward to take her hand and walk her to the rostrum outside, which had been set up for the service. As James and Kate walked down the steps of the house, with Izzy walking beside them, they walked towards the vicar and the small assembly of friends and family, and unlike most solemn weddings, there was a tumult of clapping and cheering.

As James and Kate were taking their vows and staring into each others eyes with love and affection, Ailsa and Andy held each others hand and a tear escaped down Aisla's cheek, as she said to Andy in a whisper, "Now we can rest in peace. Theirs is a marriage made in heaven. The haunting sound of the pipes being played high up on the hill above Comraich could be heard throughout the hills and glens."

James and Kate spent their honeymoon in Edinburgh at his parent's home. Kate had never been to Edinburgh before meeting James' parents, and between never ending nights of passion, she hoped that James would show her the City where he grew up. Ailsa and Andy in the mean time were staying at the farm, now that Andy had recovered from his long spell of illness. Eaden and Keith were under strict instructions from James not to allow his mother or father to lift a finger.

Over the next few months a new farm manager was installed at the farm. James and Izzy still spent time on the farm but they seemed to spend a lot more time together as a family. The first Christmas together in Comraich house set a new tradition, where James, Izzy and Kate spent all of the holidays together in Comraich as a family. Ailsa and Andy chose not to come, though they knew that they were very welcome. It was felt to be too much for Andy, who was becoming frailer. The New Year was a tradition which neither of them ever wanted to change: for Lorna, Keith, Eaden and Morag to bring the New Year in at Comraich.

The second Christmas at Comraich brought in a whole new generation: To James and Kate Wallace was born the second most beautiful little girl in the world; with jet black hair and olive skin, making her look like a little peach, Layla Wallace came into their world.

www.ingramcontent.com/pod-product-compliance
Lightning Source LLC
Chambersburg PA
CBHW070406260626
47161CB00001B/297